"Someone is trying to kill you...

"If you knew that then," Wade continued, "would you have stayed home?"

Lacey looked at him. "No. My brother's dead. I won't stop until I know why."

"I already told you. Because of me."

"Those guys out there weren't sent by you. There's more to the story. More than you even know."

"The story of my life. Ever since I found out my mother's aliases, I've been living that reality."

"This is more than just finding out if your mother was a spy, isn't it?" When Wade hesitated she said, "Please. We could be killed any second. Honesty is all we have left."

He nodded. "But that's all you're going to get out of me. Talking only gets people killed. *I* get people killed."

"But you rescued your sister—"

"Don't." He captured her gaze. His eyes glittered. "Don't make me into some hero. I opened my mouth, and she was almost killed. And the next time, your brother paid the price." His gaze darkened. "And if I can't fix this, you're next."

Katy Lee writes suspenseful romances that thrill and inspire. She believes every story should stir and satisfy the reader—from the edge of their seat. A native New Englander, Katy loves to knit warm wooly things. She enjoys traveling the side roads and exploring the locals' hideaways. A homeschooling mom of three competitive swimmers, Katy often writes from the stands while cheering them on. Visit Katy at katyleebooks.com.

Books by Katy Lee

Love Inspired Suspense

Warning Signs
Grave Danger
Sunken Treasure
Permanent Vacancy
Silent Night Pursuit

SILENT NIGHT PURSUIT

KATY LEE

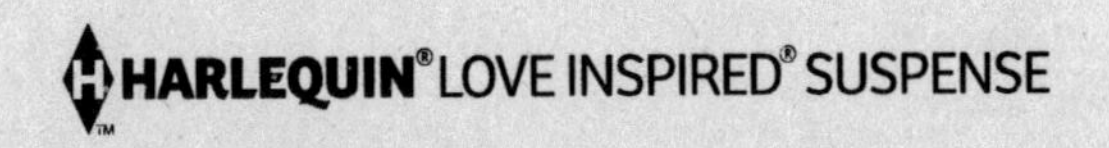

Recycling programs for this product may not exist in your area.

LOVE INSPIRED BOOKS

ISBN-13: 978-0-373-44713-8

Silent Night Pursuit

This edition published by arrangement with Love Inspired Books.

www.Harlequin.com

Printed in U.S.A.

My little children, let us not love in word, neither in tongue; but in deed and in truth.

—*1 John* 3:18

To Ben and all the other service dogs like him who assist their military handlers on a daily basis. You truly inspire.

Acknowledgments

My stories would fall flat without real-life people sharing their experiences with me. They are the true heroes behind the stories. I want to especially thank Dennis Theodore Swols, SSG United States Army. His honesty in answering my many questions about post-traumatic stress disorder as well as the amazing service dogs that have helped him in his daily life are what brought the emotions to the page. Thank you, Dennis, and thank you to your dog, Ben, too. What a blessing you have both been to my story and my life.

ONE

"In point two miles, your destination will be on your left," the GPS's mechanical voice spoke into the tension-filled interior of the old Honda Beat roadster. Lacey Phillips stole a quick glance at her rearview mirror. Blinding headlights from the car on her tail suggested she might not make it those point two miles. If this guy came any closer, she could be spending her Christmas Eve in a snowy New Hampshire ditch instead.

Not what a born-and-bred Southern girl was used to.

Lacey had nothing for warmth but a blue-jean coat and her brother's army beanie hat.

Check that: her *deceased* brother's.

"Stay on the road, Lacey," she said aloud, and tightened her hold on the wheel.

She could almost hear her brother whisper the same words to her. They'd been each other's spotter on the racetrack for so long, guiding each and every lane change from mouthpiece to earpiece, guarding against unforeseen hazards on the road ahead. Now it felt as though he guided her again. And it all started when Jeff had left her an envelope with nothing in it but a name and a key. Oh, how she wished there had been a warning of danger inside it, as well.

The car behind pulled up. For the past half hour it had kept the same taunting pace with her as when she'd spotted it outside the small town of Norcastle, New Hampshire. She'd thought it curious when they'd both took the cutoff to ascend these secluded mountain roads. Twenty more minutes of being tailgated through twists and turns and more cutoffs had caused her curiosity to change to full-on alarm.

Lacey wondered how long the car had been there before she noticed it. With her one-track mind on the sole purpose of this trip, it could have pulled up the moment she'd left work at her dad's South Carolina reconstruction race-car shop seventeen hours ago.

Get the answers was as far as her thoughts had gone when she'd found the envelope in her brother's office at the shop. Now, with her unwanted company coming up the rear, she probably should have put a little more planning into her mission. After all, her brother was dead, and she didn't believe it was an accident, as the stamp on his military file implied. How far would someone go to keep that little detail under the rug?

Lacey accelerated, hoping to find the driveway her GPS alerted her to. Somewhere in these twisty back roads and walls of thick trees was the entrance to the home of her brother's friend, Captain Wade Spencer—the name her brother had left in that envelope.

Lacey's tires slipped beneath her as the car hit ice, something she was not used to. A yank of the wheel and a downshift freed her from the skid, but she realized this two-seater Beater was not the car to take north in the beginning of winter. Reason number 345 she would never make a good wedding planner like her wise and detailed-oriented, Southern-genteel mother. It was just one more disappointment for Adelaide Phillips to lecture her daughter about when Lacey returned home.

If she returned home.

Lacey looked in the rearview mirror again and breathed a little easier with the little extra space between her car and the one behind her, but with the thoughts of her mother permeating her brain now, it wasn't too much easier.

What would Adelaide do when she heard her rebel daughter had raced off to places unknown to investigate her brother's death?

Lacey revved her engine, just as she typically did to tune her mother's sweet-as-sugar voice out of her mind. Then she floored the pedal, and her tires squealed beneath her just as they would on pit road on race day.

She had a mission, and Adelaide would just have to accept it. Lacey took some solace, though, knowing she didn't completely go alone. She believed she could step out, or drive out, as the case may be, in faith because God always went with her.

Lord, right about now, I could use a little of Your guidance and maybe some more space between me and the car behind me. They're getting awfully close again. Please, don't let them interfere with my goal. I have to make things right. Stay with me, and please cover for me with Mama, and please *help me find this Wade guy's place.*

Lacey scrutinized the dense forest ahead of her but still saw no inclination of any living being this far out from town. *Talk about cutting yourself off from the world,* she thought. *What kind of person was this Wade any—*

Lacey jolted. The car behind her had tapped her bumper! Was he playing some kind of game?

Back home on the track there might have been some words hollered out, or at the very least, an issue of a challenge for such behavior, but she didn't think for a second this guy cared about his bad sportsmanship. So what *did* he want? To stop her from getting her answers was all she could fathom.

But she needed these answers for Jeffrey, Lacey reminded herself. She wouldn't give up until her brother's life was honored, not locked up in a confidential file somewhere in DC.

The car bumped her again.

Lacey's stomach squeezed with trepidation. Never did she think she would need an exit strategy. It had always been get the answers and go home. In and out and home by Christmas dinner. End of mission.

She squeezed her steering wheel tighter and jerked when the car bumped her a third time. How she wished she'd been able to equip the Honda Beat for racing already. If she wasn't stuck in the shop working other drivers' cars, the Beat would have included at least a roll cage of tubular steel by now. Her ability to fight back would have put an end to the cat-and-mouse game this guy was playing. What was the point in tapping her bumper? Did he want her to move over?

Or to go home?

Not a chance, Lacey thought. She knew a few racers who used bullying tactics like this guy was doing. One tap meant "I'm behind you and want to come up." Two taps meant "move it, or I'll move you myself." And three taps meant "you've been warned."

So was that her third warning?

"You don't know who you're tapping, pal," she spoke into her quiet cabin. "I don't play the game for them, and I'm not playing it for you."

"Your destination is on your left." The GPS announced her arrival and Lacey flinched. Then she cringed. Apparently, she only talked big.

The GPS repeated the instructions, and Lacey flicked her blinker on. The next second, the car behind her jammed the Beat's rear bumper at full force.

The impact wrenched Lacey's neck as her head whipped back into her headrest, but she felt nothing because the looming dark abyss coming at her took precedence.

Crunches and squeals resounded as she slammed on the brakes to fight back with the car plowing her to the edge of the road. Her car turned to the right under the pressure from behind. Then before the edge neared, the strain lessened up. The guy backed off, but probably only to save himself from going over with her.

The Beat was already in a full spin. Coupled with the messy roads, the world for Lacey kept swinging round and round as she careened toward the unknown.

She gripped the wheel with one hand as she downshifted. Her headlights came back around to show a drop-off into a black void that would most likely send her down some ravine to be lost until spring.

Maybe never found at all.

Go left. The familiar voice of her brother came from the recesses of her mind. After years of his training with go-carts when she was ten years old, and cars at sixteen, she knew exactly what he would say.

One hard crank of her wheel pulled the car out of the spin and sent her back around, but unfortunately, it sent her in a skid in the opposite direction, straight at the thick, impenetrable tree line she'd been searching through before. The one with no opening, as far as she had been able to tell—and the thick tree trunks with their tentacles of bared branches coming at her said things hadn't changed. But her headlights showed something was different than before.

Where there was no sign of life before, now a dog ran straight for her, emerging from the forest.

A quick glance behind it and she caught sight of the driveway she'd been looking for. The sharp angle of Captain Wade Spencer's property was invisible to passersby, but his golden-red Labrador retriever had revealed its opening to her now as her car took aim to gun it down.

Her brake pedal plastered to the floor. The tires' skid locked their direction on their target. Lacey could do nothing but cry out to God to intervene and save the dog barreling forward.

As if by command, the animal abruptly came to a stop and sat—directly in the car's path.

"No!" Lacey shouted. That was not what she meant by intervening! At least if the dog was still running, there was a chance of it moving out of the way before impact. Now things could not get worse.

Tears blurred Lacey's vision, and wails of protest erupted from her lips. She did not want to kill this dog.

Then things got worse.

In addition to the sitting dog, a man now raced out from behind the trees, straight for the canine.

Lacey screamed louder than ever. The skid moved as if in slow motion. The whole incident couldn't have taken more than a minute from the first bump to this final skid, but in that minute she saw the devastation her impulsiveness was about to cause. If only she had thought this trip through. If only she had been more like the wise Adelaide Phillips.

If only.

Lacey closed her eyes, unable to watch the outcome to her choices, a prayer of forgiveness on her lips and regret in her heart.

* * *

Head. Check.

Feet. Check.

Arms. Check.

Wade Spencer lay in a cold, snow-filled ditch between the trees where he'd landed when he saved his dog from the out-of-control driver. All was negative with his self-exam, a routine that four tours overseas had formed into a habit. His next exam consisted of judging the well-being of Promise, his faithful dog.

Wade lifted his hand to look her over. He burrowed his fingers through her snow-covered fur for injuries. She jumped to all four paws without any problem and shook off the white flakes with little effort. His battle buddy would live to serve another day.

Now, as for the driver, he should be serving, too.

Time.

Wade gained his feet and trudged through the knee-deep snow of the ditch. He stomped up onto the road where the car spun out and came to a halt—right where Promise had been sitting under his command.

If Wade had known a car had been aiming for her, he would have commanded Promise to run, not sit. Out of the hundred and fifty commands the dog knew, any of them would have been better.

At the top of the driveway, he'd heard the car spinning out. His mind had gone to one of the many dark places of his tours where mishaps had been deadly. His feet had responsively set out to be of help in this mishap. Promise had kept up at her place beside him, but she must have thought they were playing, because she'd quickly raced ahead of him. All Wade could do was yell for her to sit. Being the good service dog she was, she did—right in front of the car.

Wade faced the hood of the heap of rust now and heard the words, "You have arrived at your destination" coming from the mechanical voice of the driver's GPS. The message nearly knocked him over again.

The driver meant to stay?

"I don't think so." Wade approached the driver's side. "This is *not* your destination. You can keep right on driving."

A woman in her late twenties sat stock-still behind the wheel, her window blown out from the tree branch she'd collided with. She wore a jean coat and a knitted cap, and her long hair, smooth as liquid chocolate, spilled out from beneath it. The GPS repeated its words again, but all Wade focused on was the terror in the woman's saucer-size eyes.

Wade pulled the car handle and swung the door wide; the tinkling of falling glass fizzled his tension a bit. The cabin light illuminated the fear in the woman's face, a pair of brown eyes shimmered and a tear spilled down her blanched cheek. He let the rest of his anger go on a grunt. "Are you hurt?"

She shook her head, but her lips trembled in silence. She squeaked out, "Are you? Or the dog? Did I k-kill the dog?"

Wade gave two sharp whistles, and Promise sidled up beside him with her tail wagging, her bushy eyebrows bouncing up and down as was her typical inquisitive way. "See for yourself."

A wail escaped the woman's lips, followed by a bucket of tears.

Wade sighed and reached for her hand to pull her out.

"I'm so sorry," she cried. "I didn't see... The car was in a skid."

"Your South Carolina plates give away your knowledge of the winters up here in New Hampshire, so I'll cut you some slack, but—"

"And someone was following me. They nearly killed me when they banged into me."

"Banged into you?" Wade searched up and down the empty street. He dropped her hand to step to the back end of the car. The dent proved her statement. "Which way did they go?"

"I don't know," she cried. "I was too busy staying on the road and not going over the ledge."

"Ledge?" Wade snapped his attention from the dark road to the very ledge that had brought the endless tunnel of darkness to his whole life. An image of another woman, his mother, dead, her neck twisted, flashed in his mind. Just one of the many images of dead people his mind remembered on a daily basis. His breathing picked up.

"Yes, the ledge. I thought I was going over it for sure." She pointed to it then grabbed her head, pulling the cap off in her anxiety. "I can still see it coming closer and closer."

Wade nearly grabbed his own head, knowing firsthand the terror she spoke of.

Except, he'd actually gone over—and lived to remember every horrifying detail.

"I need to go," he said quickly, needing to get away. "You need to go. I can't help you. Side, Promise."

He didn't need to command. Promise already stood by. Wade grabbed the bandanna tied to her collar. She should have her leash on, he admonished himself for his gaffe. The leash was his lifeline to her. Through the leash, Promise could get a read on his physiological well-being. She could sense his heart rate just by his tugs and pulls. But he'd left her leash at the house in their rush to get some fresh air away from his sister. Now he willingly rushed back to Roni's never-ending pleas for him to retire from the military and move back to New Hampshire. He'd endure her plights.

Anything but reliving that crash.

Wade's hands trembled, and vibrations shook his whole body. His hypervigilant state of mind brought on fierce shakes that had nothing to do with the frigid temperature and everything to do with the injury deep inside him. It was an injury no one could see, except for the few effects that showed on the outside.

"Wait!" the woman called on his heels. Wade picked up his steps.

"I'll call the police for you when I get to the house," he said, hoping that would suffice.

"Please, stop. I can't go anywhere until I speak with Captain Wade Spencer."

Wade tripped in the snow at her words, but the squeezing of his chest still propelled him forward. He wondered what this woman could want with him. Did one of his men need him? As captain, he needed to be there for them, even when he couldn't function himself.

"Please," she pleaded. "I can barely breathe, never mind have my faculties about me to operate a car. I really need to speak with Captain Spencer. Are you him?"

He walked on, calling out, "What do you want with Wade Spencer?"

"My brother sent me to see him."

"Who's your brother?"

"Jeff Phillips."

"Liar." Wade whipped around to face her, now ready to fight instead of take flight. In a hypervigilant state, either worked.

Promise didn't miss a beat. She sat at attention by his side, eyes sharp, body poised for her next instructions.

"I'm not lying. He told me to come." The woman's lips trembled.

"He's dead, so he couldn't have told you anything."

Her face crumpled right before him. Her soft features grew taut. She grabbed at her chest, and he wondered if she felt what he experienced. He hoped not. He didn't wish the debilitation of PTSD on anyone.

She dropped her hand to her stomach and wrapped it around her midriff. "I don't think I'll ever fully accept those words. Jeff's been dead for three weeks, and it still doesn't compute." She swiped a palm across her eyes. "Can you just tell me where I can find Wade Spencer?"

Wade felt his hands shaking. Promise noticed, too. As was her special way, she pushed her soft and firm head into his palm. He latched on like a drowning victim, digging his fingers deep. A few strokes across her fur and air slowly filtered into his lungs again. The vise in his chest released a bit of its pressure, but his clenched jaw stayed in its grip.

"I'm Wade," he admitted between his teeth, still petting Promise.

"Oh, I'm so glad I made it." She sniffed. "I was beginning to think you didn't exist. That my brother made you up."

"I exist." *Barely.* His chest constricted again.

"My brother's death wasn't an accident. I just know it. The army passed me off from one official to another, and they all have the same lame story. A mechanical issue on an engine he was working on." She sputtered as if the words made her laugh. "*My* brother, mechanic extraordinaire, had a mechanical malfunction that blew up in his face. What a joke."

Wade's whole body rocked from a tremble, starting from his feet straight up to his shoulders. "It's no joke. It's the truth." Promise whined, and Wade knew it was because he was breathing heavy. "It's best if you keep your nose out of where it doesn't belong and go home."

Wade left her there with her mouth agape. He needed to get away before he lost all control over his body and writhed on the ground before her. Besides, he didn't believe the lame story the military offered about her brother, either, and that meant what she didn't know could save her life.

"Please..." She was back to playing his shadow. "Jeff was killed on purpose, wasn't he? Just tell me, Mr. Spencer. Who killed him?"

Wade halted and spun around. "I did!" His chest heaved up and down. "And unless you want to die, too, you'll do as I say and go home." If that didn't make her disappear, nothing would.

The swishing of her shoes in the snow didn't follow him this time. He walked alone with his service dog. At the bend he gave one last look and found the driveway empty except for the footprints she'd left behind.

Mission accomplished.

He continued on his way, but before he could take two more steps, a blast shot into the night. Wade flew to the ground, hunting for cover like so many times before. He sought the dark forest in all directions for a sniper as the gunshot echoed back at him through the trees.

The terrors of combat banged into Wade's head just as the reverberating sound of the explosion had thrown him further than to the ground. It had sent him back to battles he wished to forget but knew he never would. No longer did he feel the frozen snow beneath his face and hands, but instead it was the hot dusty sand of his tours overseas that took control of his mind.

Wade reached behind him for the gun in his waist holster as he peered up and around looking for the enemy. The snowcapped trees brought him back to reality.

No desert.

No sniper.

Instead, it was Jeff Phillips's sister who'd come to hunt him down.

He could only think that it was the woman who'd taken the shot at him. She was the only one around, and he had just told her he killed her brother. It made sense she'd take him out now.

Another report wrenched through the air. Immediately, the sound of a car speeding away followed. Both sources came from below at the road and not around him—or at him.

Phillips's kid sister wasn't shooting at him after all, he surmised. But if he wasn't wearing the bull's-eye, then who was?

She was.

Wade jumped to his feet and shot off back down the driveway. Promise raced along beside him. He would have liked to tell Promise to get to the girl's side, but his dog was trained to assist him, not anyone else.

Snow flew up in a cloud around them. Down the road around the bend, the woman's car lights still beamed. Her driver's door stood wide and the car was where she'd left it. But she was nowhere in sight.

A quick survey bounced his vision from tree to tree, ditch to ditch, rock to rock. And there he located her, crouched low behind a boulder.

Wade rushed to the rock and dropped to his knees. He reholstered his gun behind him as he studied the way she held the shoulder of her jean coat in severe silence. No screams. No agony of pain. Just startled shock before cognition filtered in.

She'd been shot.

He removed her stiff, sticky hand from where a dark blotch of blood blossomed. At the same time he scanned the area behind the rock. Had the gunman been in the car that drove away? Or was there a second one waiting in the trees to get another shot off when the woman emerged from her hiding place? With the darkness, Wade couldn't be sure. But he also couldn't leave her here to bleed to death. The thin jean coat's fabric was shredded on the arm, but still he couldn't tell if the shot had been taken in her arm or upper chest. He wouldn't know until he got her to the house.

The trip called for a calculated plan of action. The driver's-side window of her car was blown out, but the car should still move. Wade judged the distance to the Beat and made the decision that he could drive her up to the house a lot faster than run her up. Plus, he didn't need to give the shooter more target practice if he was still in the area.

With his plan set, Wade untied Promise's bandanna and stuffed it into the woman's coat. "Hold this there while I lift you."

"Get away from me," she said, pushing at him with barely enough strength to shoo a fly.

"All in due time, Ms. Phillips." He lifted her and made the run for the waiting vehicle.

"I don't want to go anywhere with you! You killed my brother!"

He ignored her protests and carried out his self-imposed orders. "Promise, to the house," he commanded the dog. Wade ducked his upper body over the woman's and charged for the car. He placed her quickly but gently through to the passenger seat from the driver's side. No more bullets sprayed them, and Wade took that to mean the shooter had been a drive-by and not in the woods. But his plan of action never lost momentum. Mere seconds went by before he had the car in gear and speeding up the inclined drive through the woods that led to the main house.

"I said I don't want to go anywhere with you. I hate you!" Her head dropped back and he could see her jaw clench. She'd yet to even whimper in pain.

"Hate me all you want. I'm fine with that. It tells me you still have some fight left in you."

"You're right, and I'm going to make you pay for what you did."

They reached the house, and Wade took the circle around the empty fountain, shut down for the season. He pulled up to the front entrance and had barely put the car in Park before he jumped out and ran around to the passenger side. The fool girl already had the door open, trying to exit the car. He scooped her up again, ignoring her struggles up the steps.

"Put me down!" Now she cried, but not from pain. He knew the sound of guilty pain. She hated herself more for having to depend on the man who'd caused her brother's death.

"You have no choice but to let me help you now, Ms. Phillips. You're on my family's property." He turned the knob to the double front doors and kicked them wide. "That makes me responsible for you, and there's no way I'm letting another person die because of me."

TWO

A woman who had a few years on Lacey's twenty-seven and a lot more fashion sense rushed down a long foyer. A green silk scarf wrapped around her neck fluttered behind her along with her flowing red hair. Lacey saw glitz and glamour racing toward her, or maybe it was the crystal chandelier sparkling down on the lady. Either way, Lacey didn't care who she was as long as she wasn't Wade Spencer.

Lacey pushed at the man still holding her in his arms. She moaned through the burn at her shoulder but kept her face averted, unwilling to give him even a glint of attention.

"Roni," he called over her head. "She took a bullet. I need to lay her down."

Surprise quickly washed away to efficiency on the fancy lady's face. "It'll be faster to use Cora's room down here than to take her upstairs. Follow me."

They stormed through two living rooms and entered a huge dining room with more crystal bling. An older woman was setting the table with white-and-gold china. Her maid outfit said she wasn't the mother of the house. She nearly dropped the plate when they stormed through.

"Cora, we're using your room," Roni said as she

passed down the long table. "Call 911 and tell them someone's been shot."

A shocked Cora put the plate down and reached for her phone in her apron pocket. As Lacey was carried past her, she said, "God bless you, my dear." Lacey could hear her talking to the dispatcher before they hit an enormous stainless-steel kitchen. She wondered where the bedrooms were if they deemed this course faster. The immensity of the place didn't constitute a house but a mansion.

It would appear her brother's killer wasn't hurting.

"What's her name?" Roni called over her shoulder.

"Ms. Phillips," Wade said.

"Lacey," Lacey answered in unison. "And I don't need *him* speaking for me."

"Whoa." The woman shot a glance over her shoulder, the arches of her red sculpted eyebrows nearly reaching the twelve-foot-high ceilings. "Did *you* shoot this woman, Wade?"

"Of course not," he answered.

With a look of doubt, Roni led them to the next room. "Lay her on the bed. *Gently.* Good. Now, where's your gun?"

"I said I didn't shoot her," Wade retorted over Lacey.

"And *I* said, where's your gun?" Roni spoke clearly and forcefully right back at him from the other side.

Wade clamped his jaw tight, but in the next second he reached behind his back and withdrew a .38 caliber from the waistband. He dropped it into the bedside-table drawer with an "are you happy now?" look.

Lacey sensed the argument going on above her was a common one between the two of them. For some reason, Roni didn't want Wade carrying. Did Roni know about Wade's past offenses?

Before Lacey could ask, pain exploded from her arm. Roni brought Lacey's coat down the injured arm.

Lacey hissed in response, then through gritted teeth said, "It doesn't matter if he carries or not, you know. He goes for a more secretive and calculated way of bumping people off." She sneered at the man on her right and got her first real glimpse of him in full light.

Jet-black hair in a military cut, electric-blue eyes in a well-shaven face, a dimple on the right cheek even without a smile.

"He knows it's not other people I'm worried about," Roni said, pulling Lacey's attention back to her.

Lacey grew quiet at her remark. If not other people, then who?

Himself?

She took in the six-foot-tall man. His face gave nothing away, but his muscles beneath his black T-shirt tensed and shook. Was it from more than adrenaline?

Snip...snip...

Lacey shot a look back at Roni. She was cutting the sleeve of Lacey's cotton sweater, starting from the wrist up.

"Hey! Can you make him leave first?"

Roni cast her matching blue eyes over to Wade. "I've bandaged enough wounds. Why don't you check on Cora."

"Not a bullet wound, you haven't. I know what to do. You don't. I'm not going anywhere until I've assessed the injury."

Lacey cut in, "Except I don't want you anywhere near me."

He crossed his strong arms at his chest as his reply. His stolid face expressed no emotion as flawlessly as a Westminster guard on duty. The idea of the wolf guarding the henhouse nearly made her laugh. Then Lacey screamed out in pain as Roni's fingers met wounded flesh on her upper arm.

As Wade leaned across Lacey to inspect the area, his woodsy aftershave lingered in her face. She inhaled, then held her breath, partly to not smell any more of him, partly to keep in what she already had. She cringed at her softness. So what if he smelled good. It didn't change the fact that he had blood on his hands.

After a quick nod, Wade's gaze dropped down from above her. Mere inches away, he said, "You'll live."

"Don't look so happy about it."

He didn't even blink at her remark, but he did slowly pull away. "You said someone had been following you. When did you notice them?"

Lacey sobered as she remembered her drive in. Roni's opening of the first-aid kit became a focal point. "When I entered Norcastle. It was when they took the turnoff to come up here with me that I thought it strange two people would be traveling this far out at the same time. But they didn't try to kill me until..." Lacey glanced at Wade. Maybe the incident had something to do with this man, and that was why he was so concerned. He was trying to cover his tracks.

"Continue."

Lacey hesitated sharing any more while being unprotected in the man's house. "Can't this wait for the police?"

"I'll need to give them as many details as I can. They'll need to know how to proceed."

"What other information would they possibly need other than someone took shots at me?"

"Like why you think they took shots at you. Now tell me, they didn't try to kill you until when?"

Lacey lifted her chin. Since when did she hold back?

"Fine. They plowed into me when I put my blinker on to turn into *your* driveway. Are you sure they weren't friends of yours? Or rather, enemies? You must have a long list of them. I know I'm on it."

"Our driveway?" Roni piped up. "And what enemies? What is she talking about, Wade?"

Wade raised a hand to silence Roni. "Just get her cleaned up. We'll talk later." He walked to the window and peered out.

Or perhaps he was looking for those enemies he refused to talk about.

He closed the blinds and stepped back against the wall. His folded arms at his chest exposed the strong, lean muscles that had lifted her with ease moments before, but now walled him off from everyone in the room.

The man was hiding something.

A stinging pain pulled Lacey's attention back to her arm with a sharp inhale.

Roni swabbed her wound with an alcohol wipe. "It's a bad graze. It'll most likely leave a scar. But I've always said there's nothing wrong with scars." She reached up with one hand in a latex glove that Lacey hadn't even seen her put on. Blood covered the fingers.

Her blood.

As Lacey's stomach dropped at the sight, Roni reached for the scarf at her neck without thought to soiling it. She pulled it free to reveal what lay beneath it.

Scars.

Puckered and mutilated skin gave way to a fiery incident that took Lacey's mind off her own wound to question Roni's.

"What happened?"

"A car accident when we were kids."

"That's enough, Roni." Wade gave a single shake of

his head to end their conversation. A dare to defy him went out.

The heavy feeling of secrecy filled the room. It seemed Wade Spencer's life revolved around more than one. But then when one of them was murder, it was only natural to have a lifetime of other cover-ups.

"More secrets, Mr.—" She stopped because her attention was pulled from the granitelike man against the wall down to his legs.

He literally shook in his combat boots. The man may think he stood impassive, but his own body turned traitor on him and gave his guilty secrets away. Before she could call him out on his guilt, the dog placed her paw on his thigh and pressed her head into his arm, nudging harder and harder until his hand reached to pet her head. He moved over her fur, first slowly, then with more purpose. When Lacey looked back at his legs, they had returned to a state of stability.

The dog wasn't a typical pet, she realized.

"How'd she do that?" Lacey asked, not pretending what she saw didn't really happen. Her mother would say she was being rude for speaking out of turn, but Lacey didn't feel like being proper at the moment. She'd just escaped death and was looking at the man responsible for her brother's.

"You ask too many questions," Wade replied. "That's probably what got you into this mess."

"Wade, knock it off," Roni cut in. "Promise is a service dog. The army is experimenting with trained dogs to help soldiers with post-traumatic stress disorder. They sent my brother home with her to help him—"

"I said, that's enough!" Wade retreated from the room on a pivot. His tense, muscled back turned the corner of the kitchen and disappeared.

Now Lacey understood Roni's concern about Wade carrying a weapon.

And *she* was pushing him too far with her questions.

Lacey watched Roni's eyelashes fall over her eyes in sadness. "I'm sorry if I overstepped my bounds. My mother has tried to teach me to be a lady, but I've yet to live up to any of her ideals, all ten thousand of them. But it's not for lack of trying. I really am sorry."

Roni smiled weakly but accepted Lacey's apology.

"So Wade is your brother?"

"Yes." The fashionable woman taped the bandage up like a pro, not a bit of queasiness or whining like some sissy girl. Proof never to judge a book by its cover. Roni approached a dresser and pulled out an oversize blouse with tiny yellow flowers.

Lacey cringed. "Cora's?"

"She won't mind, and it'll be loose enough to put on with ease."

"I suppose, but I don't do clothes with flowers."

"What's wrong with flowers?" Roni asked as she removed the rest of Lacey's trashed sweater and carefully inserted her arms through the sleeves.

"Nothing's wrong with flowers for some girls, like my mother. And maybe you, but the guys at the racetrack would never let me live it down."

Roni's hands stilled with her task. "You race?"

"Sometimes. It can be hard to be taken seriously as a girl behind the wheel."

"Tell me about it," Roni agreed with a smirk. "I'm co-owner of a track and it can be tough. What do you race?"

"I'm in the process of reconstructing a Beat roadster for my next car. Or I was up until I smashed at the end of your driveway. I'm more of a spotter for my brother..." Lacey's voice caught at the mention of Jeffrey. "It was easier when he was home. Without him to vouch for me, I spend most of my days in the shop working on the cars instead. He was my biggest supporter. And now he's… gone."

"Where'd he go?" Roni fitted the buttons up the front.

"Army."

Her hands stilled. "When does he come home next?"

"He's not coming home. Ever." Lacey felt her lips tremble as Roni put the words together.

She dropped back. "Oh, Lacey, I'm so sorry."

Roni sat on the side of the bed, her eyes filled. She gave a quick look toward the door. Lacey knew thoughts of her own brother filled her mind. As much as Lacey wanted to hate the woman for being grateful for not losing Wade when Jeff was gone forever, especially since Wade had a part in Jeff's death, as he'd admitted to, she couldn't hate Roni.

"It's okay if you want to thank God for bringing your brother home. It won't upset me. From one sister to another, I get it. If Jeffrey had survived, I would be jumping for joy, no matter who watched." She looked at her injured arm. "And I definitely wouldn't have been here getting shot at on Christmas Eve. I guess I shouldn't have come. Once again, my mother was right, and I failed to heed her wise teachings. Why is thinking things through so hard?"

"I don't understand." Roni tilted her head.

Lacey shrugged. "I disappoint my mama pretty much every day. I'll never be like her and think like her."

"No. I mean, how would your brother coming home from the army have prevented you from being shot?"

"Oh, easy. Because I wouldn't have come here looking for his killer."

Roni's long lashes lifted high. "His killer is *here*?"

Wade appeared in the doorway with an older man, halting Lacey from explaining further about Wade's involvement.

Lacey considered blurting out the truth anyway. She looked at the men, but before she opened her mouth, her mother's annoying voice filled her mind. *Think before you speak, Lacey, dear.* Her thick Southern drawl with its inflection of disappointment came through loud and clear.

Lacey held her tongue and looked at Wade. His searing eyes said he waited for her to make her decision, too. Would she take the opportunity to spill his secret in front of his sister and whoever the older man beside him was? Their dad, probably.

Seconds ticked by as the three people stared at the poor wounded girl.

Poor being the operative word. Wade Spencer was loaded. Which meant he could buy his way out of any case brought against him. She didn't stand a chance of getting her answers from Mr. Secrets the legit way.

Her hand went to her neck and fiddled with the key clasped there beneath the flowered blouse. She'd put it on her chain when she removed it from her brother's envelope yesterday. This key would unlock the answers she came for.

And Wade Spencer would be the one to give them to her.

Lacey turned away from Wade to answer Roni. "Jeff's killer is around somewhere. He can't hide forever."

"What a way to spend Christmas Eve, wouldn't you say, Miss Phillips?" The older gentleman Lacey had thought was Wade's father, but turned out to be an uncle, entered the room again. Wade and Roni were seeing the lawmen out, so that left her alone for the time being.

"It's Lacey, and I'm sorry I messed up your holiday. You must think I'm so rude coming here tonight."

When the police had questioned her earlier, Wade's uncle had leaned against the wall and heard why she'd made this trip. She'd left out the part of Wade's confession, but told them about her brother's so-called accident in the army and how she'd come to talk to her brother's friend.

The uncle stepped up to where Lacey sat on the edge of the bed. He offered his hand for a warm shake. "Clay Spencer. The kids' dad, Bobby, was my little brother. And don't you worry about what we think. You're hurting. We all feel your pain and frustration, especially with your car being taken in to be processed as evidence. You probably won't make it back for Christmas dinner with your family."

The realization lifted her chin. The older man offered a sweet, supportive smile as though he understood her dilemma, but he also wore a very nice suit with a festive holiday tie and a red silk handkerchief in his breast pocket. He'd come here tonight to spend Christmas Eve with his family, and she had intruded.

Lacey cringed at her impulsiveness to jump into her car and head north without any thought to what day she would be arriving on Wade Spencer's doorstep. What had she thought he would do? Welcome her in to celebrate with his family?

No. The fact was she didn't think at all. At least nothing but what she'd come for.

"You stay as long as you need to," the uncle invited warmly.

Lacey gave a weak laugh. "You seem to have a better grasp at this hospitality thing than this Southern girl does."

The man smiled big. "I do love a good party, and the more the merrier. But seriously, the kids have plenty of room. Plus, I don't think Wade's going to let you go anywhere tonight. He told the chief of police he would take care of getting you home. He feels responsible for you since this incident happened on his family's property."

"This gigantic place is his family's?"

"Technically his and Veronica's, Roni's, now. They lost their parents years ago. Only Roni lives here, though. Wade lives on base in Virginia. He's only home for the holidays. I used to live here after their parents died, but once Veronica was of age, I moved to the empty caretaker's house on the pond, a little ways into the property, then eventually I moved into town. Let's just say Veronica and I don't always get along, even in ten thousand square feet. Even on thousands of acres. Moving off the property was best. Besides, I like it better in town. Great house for social gatherings with my friends. And speaking of friends, I have a few in influential places who might be able to help you uncover some information about your brother."

"What kind of friends?"

"Lawyers, politicians, PIs, you name it. One can never have too many circles, I say. I'm sure one of them could look into the possibility of a cover-up."

A spark of excitement ignited but quickly died out. What if those people were Wade's friends? Who would they be loyal to then? "No, I've talked to enough official people to know they're not much help to me, but thank you."

"Just let me know if you change your mind and want to talk privately with someone. I can make it happen."

"For now, I just want to talk to Wade. I'll wait here for him. I don't dare try to find him in this place. I'm directionally challenged and might get lost."

Clay laughed. "You don't know the half of it. Bobby married well, but his wife, Meredith, was also a bit paranoid. When I moved in after the accident to care for the kids, I found all these secret passages she had built. Creepy, for sure."

Lacey checked the adjoining room and saw no one approached. She was really only looking for Mr. Secrets before she asked for more pieces about his past. She would need all the details she could round up. "Roni's scars. She mentioned something about an accident causing them. Is that how their parents died, too?"

"Yes, it was a horrifying accident. Just a horrible accident. Bobby and Meredith perished, as well as their eighteen-month-old son Luke."

Lacey frowned at the thought of the baby dying, too.

"Veronica was scarred in the fire and would have died as well if Wade hadn't pulled her out and away from the car before it fully exploded. They'd gone over the ledge on the road out front."

"Ledge?" Now Lacey sounded the way Wade had when she'd told him she'd nearly gone over it. All snooping came to a halt. What was left of her blood ran cold. Wade and his family had gone over the same ledge she had just brushed death with. "When?" was all she could ask.

"It's been twenty-eight years now. Hard to believe, but Wade was eight and Veronica was three. He got her to safety, but being this far out from town and so far from the house, there was nothing else he could do for the rest of his family."

"Of course not. I doubt an adult could, never mind a

child." Lacey thought this was possibly why Wade had told her to go home when she said she'd nearly gone over the ledge. It had probably brought back horrible memories of his accident. Had that been why he'd told her he killed Jeff? To get rid of her before she saw him fall apart? His bouncing legs could have been an indication that the crash affected his PTSD just as much as his years in combat did. "And you stepped in to raise them."

"Moved right in. There was no reason to take them from the only home they knew. I also helped with the business Bobby and Meredith started. It seemed only right to keep that going for the kids."

"The racetrack?"

"Spencer Speedway. How'd you know?"

"Roni mentioned it. My family owns a reconstruction race-car shop, so that's probably why Jeff and Wade hit it off as friends. They had racing in common."

"I don't think so. Wade wants nothing to do with racing. He asked me to stay on as CEO for him so he could leave town and be an army man at eighteen. There had to be something else that brought them together, because it couldn't be racing."

"Huh, I just figured." She shrugged, then inhaled sharply from the pain.

Clay gave a slow whistle. "Painkillers kicking in yet?"

"Slowly."

"Here, you should have that in a sling." Clay withdrew his red handkerchief from his suit-coat breast pocket and knotted it into a quick sling. Gently he placed her injured arm in it. "That should hold it still and cause less pain. You up for a walk?"

Lacey stood from the bedside and tested her head. No light-headedness, a good sign she'd live to ride another day. "Where are we off to?"

"Just to the garage. You being a track rat and all, I thought you might like to see the collection we have in the showcase."

"Showcase? That sounds intriguing. What might I see in your showcase? Any roadsters?"

Clay broke into his big comforting grin again. "Right this way. Your chariot awaits." He took his suit coat off and draped it over Lacey's shoulders. He led her through the kitchen, but in the other direction from where she'd entered. Out the door and across a snow-covered patio, a glass-enclosed building stood. One flick and the structure illuminated. The gray-painted concrete floor shined so clean and bright one could eat off it. A priceless collection of cars from vintage to modern were parked at various angles. Clay or Roni obviously had added a few, like the stunning cherry-red Ferrari F40 front and center.

"If only Jeff could see this..." She stuttered on the ripping pain through her chest that usurped the one in her arm tenfold. She wondered when she would stop forgetting her brother was dead.

"Are you well, Lacey?" Clay asked as he searched her face.

"I've been better, but it's got nothing to do with my arm." She blew out a breath. "So where's that roadster?"

"Right over here." He led her around back to where a small black British roadster sparkled clean and restored.

"Do you ever take her out? On the track, I mean."

"The speedway offers certain days of the year when people can unleash their babies. Come spring, you must give her a spin."

"Me? Is she yours?"

"Technically, she belonged to Meredith. Like I said, Bobby married well. Meredith's father gave them the land for the track as a wedding gift as well as this side of the mountain for a home. But now the kids own it all. Including the cars you see here. Veronica drives them, but Wade doesn't touch them."

"So he doesn't like racing or cars?"

"Hey, Questions! What are you doing out here?" Wade stood in the entrance, a sandy camouflage army coat half on, half off. His chest rose and fell as though he'd run out to her. "Are you *crazy*? You were just shot at. You up for another round?"

Clay stepped up with his hands raised. "Don't yell at her. It was my idea. We got to talking about cars, and I thought...well, I guess I didn't think at all."

"The conversation's over," Wade said to his uncle, but his eyes locked on Lacey.

"I'll just go in and see if Veronica and Cora need some help with dinner." Clay escaped the room without a reply from anyone.

"Hey, Secrets, you didn't have to be so rude," Lacey spouted. "Your uncle was just trying to take my mind off my pain. What are you so hushed up about anyway?"

"The walls have ears, and you never know who's listening. You want to know what happened to Jeff? *That's* what happened to him."

Her first clue had come when she least expected it. Lacey snapped to attention, nearly sputtering when she asked, "What was he saying? Who was listening?"

Wade's eyes jumped from window to window as though he was trying to see out into the darkness beyond the glass. If Lacey hadn't been shot at and nearly pushed over a cliff tonight, she would say this man was paranoid and uttering conspiracy-theory nonsense. But under the circumstances, she looked out the windows, too.

"I'm sending you home on a plane tomorrow," he said.

"You are not to come back. Ever. Live your life. It's what your brother would want you to do."

"Shows you what you know. My brother left me something with a note with your name on it. That tells me I'm doing exactly what he would want me to do. Find the answers."

"What'd he leave you?"

"This." Lacey reached into her blouse and pulled out a long chain with the small key dangling from it.

All in the same breath, Wade yanked her arm toward him as the glass around them shattered into millions of pieces.

Lacey landed on a thud and realized it was Wade's hard chest. He'd brought her down with him in a maneuver that had saved her life. It was as though he knew she'd made herself a target…again. She looked up to see the shattered windshield of the British roadster behind her, right where she'd been standing.

Another blast and more shattering deafened her ears. Lacey covered her head with her arms as Wade moved her to the floor. He dragged himself along the concrete on his elbows to the wall and a safe. After a few turns of the lock, the door opened to show rows of keys. He grabbed a set and shimmied back to her as Promise came through the door, crouched low on her haunches, as well. As soon as she saw her handler, she took up her post beside him.

"Stay low and get to the Ferrari," he ordered.

Lacey followed without complaint.

Bullets came from both the front and back. Car windows exploded around them. Whoever the goons were, they had the house surrounded and didn't plan on leaving anything or anyone in one piece.

Wade opened the door and Lacey crawled through, keeping her body down as she crossed over the driver's seat. Promise found her place on the floor of the front seat, and Wade got behind the wheel. As soon as he had the car started, he had it in gear and flying out through the broken glass.

Bullets hit the car, but he tore down the driveway and out onto the road in a flash. He couldn't have picked a better vehicle, Lacey thought. It went sixty miles an hour in 3.9 seconds. They would be out of these woods in no time.

Except when they hit the road, Wade actually slowed down.

He reached into one of the many pockets on his army combat coat and pulled out a cell phone. One tap of a number dialed someone, and immediately Roni could be heard yelling.

Wade stopped her and said, "We're okay. Stay in the safe room and call the police. Don't worry about us. You got this, Roni." He clicked off and pocketed the phone.

He drove in silence, obviously not willing to elaborate about what a safe room was…and why he had one. Lacey could only figure it was one of those secret passages Clay had mentioned to her. At least Roni, Clay and Cora would be safe, if the room lived up to its title. That only left her and Wade out in the open.

She searched through the rear window, but it remained dark and empty. Even still, she asked, "Can't you go a little faster?"

"It's not always about speed," he replied.

She sputtered. "Yes, it is."

After a quick, tacit look her way, he went back to giving the road his full attention, conversation over.

As they passed through the quiet little town of Norcastle, Lacey noticed the sparkling colored lights strung from some of the old storefronts and homes. In her nervous ride into town earlier, she hadn't paid much attention. Now she speculated with the huge factories along the river that Norcastle had once been an old mill town. The mill buildings looked to be lit up as apartments now. The town obviously had seen some reconstruction after a period of low economic times, but they seemed to be flourishing better now. Before Lacey could ask about it, Wade took a turn for the interstate.

"Where are we going?"

"Virginia," he answered, short but not sweet.

"What's in Virginia? Is that where the musclemen are from?"

"No. It's where I'm from. And it's also where the locker is that your key, or I should say *my* key, belongs to. Buckle up. We have a long drive."

Lacey peered over at the speedometer and rolled her eyes. "At the speed you're going, you're right. This could take forever."

THREE

"Merry Christmas." Wade pulled away from the drive-through doughnut shop, passing over a steaming paper cup to Lacey. Her long dark lashes blinked over her sleep-fogged eyes as she roused from her slumber with a wide yawn. She looked at the cup in his hand quizzically. "Coffee," he said. "Black. I figured that's the way you liked it."

She arched a dark eyebrow at his presumption of her drink tastes, but quickly unhooked her arm from his uncle's makeshift sling so she could grab the warm cup in both hands. She averted her gaze to the passenger window while she sipped. Her deep sigh proved he'd been dead on about the not-so-dainty Lacey's coffee tastes.

"Thank you," she mumbled after another sip, her deep Southern voice resonating through the cabin. Such a strong voice for a small woman, he thought. But it was good that she was small. As it was, her legs were plastered to the door because Promise and her seventy-pound frame took up most of the confined space. Wade was glad to see Lacey give the dog room, even if that meant an uncomfortable ride for herself. "And I guess I should say Merry Christmas to you, too. I suppose this is not how you planned on spending the holiday, or your military leave, for that matter. Not that I care." She turned his way, her chin lifted. "Because I don't."

With his view to the road, he hoped she couldn't see him suppress a smile. "Of course not. Why would you? But let me set the record straight, just so you don't lose any more sleep over my missed holiday, while you're not caring, of course. They're not my plans. They're my sister's. I'd just as soon have stayed on base. So *my* plans didn't work out anyway this year."

"I always say making plans is useless," she said, taking another sip. "Just go unless God tells you no. That's my motto."

Wade huffed at her silly remark. "No offense, Lacey, but I don't think your *motto's* working for you."

"Offense taken. You don't know anything about me." She took off the handkerchief and tossed it at him. He picked it up off his lap and stuffed it into his combat jacket's bottom-right pocket. Apparently, he'd touched on some nerve, but why stop there?

"I know all I need to know about you. You came north on Christmas Eve with nothing but a key and not a thought to what you might be venturing into. You were nearly killed because of your 'just go' motto, and yet, you put yourself right back into the line of fire for a glimpse at some shiny cars. In the army, we have a term for people like you. *Liability*."

"Now, see, I like to think of it more as quick-witted. After all, you're here right where I wanted you. When I showed up on your doorstep, you weren't going to give me the time of day. Just admit it. 'Go home,' you said. Now you're stuck in a car with me while I interrogate you to my heart's content. I'd say my motto is working out just fine." She blew at the steaming cup and turned to her window, mumbling, "Just don't tell my mother."

Wade eyed the back of her silky hair. It was knotted a bit from sleeping on it all night. He wished he had a comb for her. A cough escaped his throat at his outlandish thought. Promise lifted her head to assess his well-being. To assure her he was fine, Wade jumped back into the conversation. "Your mom doesn't see things your way, I take it. I think I like her."

"You would." Lacey swung to face him again. Her hair fell in a huge chocolaty curl over her shoulder.

Again with the hair, he thought. He was so used to grooming Promise on a daily basis, he must be going soft.

Lacey put out her free hand. "Speaking of which, may I use your phone? My parents are going to be expecting me for Christmas dinner tonight, and I don't see that happening now."

Wade's attention drifted from her outstretched hand to her expectant face as her words registered. When they did, he barked out a laugh. "See what I mean? Your motto's not working for you. You thought you'd be home for Christmas dinner after driving up the East Coast one day and back down the next? That made sense to you?"

She pursed her lips in irritation. "Just give me the phone."

"Can't. Chucked it."

Her hand dropped. "What do you mean you chucked it?"

"It's called Planning Ahead 101. Let me enlighten you. These aren't your street gangs doing drive-bys. For us to move forward safely, we must think strategically not only with our strategies, but theirs. That means lose anything they can even remotely trace us with. So sayonara, phone."

Lacey put her coffee in the cup holder and sagged against the hand-stitched leather seat with a sound of defeat. Promise, sensing turmoil around her, immediately stirred and pushed to a sitting position. Wade reached out to touch her so she would feel that he was fine, but before he did, Promise brought her paws to Lacey's lap and rested there with imploring eyes.

Wade felt his mouth drop. Promise had never tried to comfort anyone besides him. Wade wasn't jealous; he was just surprised. He watched to see if it would work, and sure enough, a few absent strokes from Lacey and Promise had succeeded with her mission—to calm her down.

And Lacey didn't even realize it.

That part Wade was jealous of. He wished Promise always succeeded with him like that, but there were times…

"Fine." Lacey broke into Wade's dispiriting thoughts. "I get it. Phone's gone. It's for our own protection. I'll find a pay phone or something."

"Your parents' phone most likely has a trace. You can't call anyone."

Lacey's face crumpled in an instant. "You're serious. This is bad."

"Your brother is dead. You tell me."

Lacey glanced out the window to the late-morning sun rising up from Virginia's eastern seaboard. "I can't tell you anything because *you* won't tell *me* anything. How can I plan ahead when all I have is a key?"

"All right, Questions. What do you want to know?"

"First, I want to know who these people chasing me are."

"I don't have that answer because I, myself, don't know."

"Then, how do you know they can track us?"

"Because they found your brother when it was his business not to be found. Your brother was a research analyst in the United States Army's counterintelligence department. Do you know what that entails? Let me enlighten you. Gathering intelligence under the radar."

"So you think he died because of something he knew."

"I *know* he died because of something he knew."

"Did it have something to do with the army?"

"No. It had something to do with me. I meant it when I said I killed him. I may not have caused the explosion, but I set the fuse when I asked him for help." Wade gripped the steering wheel and took the next turn for a parking area. He shut the car down and kept his eyes in the rearview mirror. After thirty seconds, a black Lincoln slowly drove by. He kept the info to himself. No need to cause Lacey to make more panicked decisions. She may think she made her choices calm and collected, or quick-witted, as she touted, but her past choices weren't life-and-death as they were now.

"Where are we?" she asked.

"Train station. There's a locker inside that the key belongs to. Jeff and I used it as a dead drop."

"What's that?"

"When two people want to pass information to one another without being seen together, they can establish a place to leave the intel."

"Intel? Why does this all sound like some sort of spy mission? Wait. Was Jeff a *spy*?" The idea looked as if it was about to make her head implode. Wade knew the feeling.

"Not Jeff. He was just helping me get information on the side." Wade swallowed hard. Once he told Lacey all he knew, she would be in so much danger. But as of last night, she was a target anyway. Whether she knew it or not, she was a dead woman by just being near him. "Your brother wasn't the spy, Lacey. The spy was my mother.

And apparently, she's still killing people from her grave. I'm sorry to tell you this, but you're most likely next."

Wade's mother was a *spy*? For whom? Lacey puzzled over this while they hustled toward the train station. She had never known anyone who was a spy, or even knew someone who knew someone. She supposed they were out there, but that world was so far out of her reality, it seemed as if it belonged to Hollywood. Except the bullets that came her way last night weren't blanks, and for someone to use real bullets on her, they obviously didn't want some secret to get out. She wished she could tell them she didn't know anything, their secrets were safe. But she supposed now she did know something and that made her a liability to someone.

Liability. Just as Wade had referred to her. She didn't want to let on, but his term for her hit hard. How many times had she heard her mother say Lacey would be the death of her?

Lacey swallowed hard and put it out of her mind for Wade's ogre of a mother instead. "So all this cloak-and-dagger stuff has to do with your mom?"

"Not here," Wade said with his hand at her lower back, pushing her toward the entrance. "We'll talk later."

Concern saturated his voice. She glanced back to see him searching the road to his left. "Are the shooters here? Did they find us? It was probably your driving. You should let me drive next time."

"There won't be a next time if we don't keep moving."

Lacey ducked deeper behind the collar of Clay's suit coat as she picked up her step.

Promise barreled along with her, matching her stride, protecting her like a guard. Wade hadn't even had to tell her to do so, the dog was so smart.

They reached the entrance door, but at someone's yell to "Stop right there!" they halted in their tracks.

Lacey shot a look to her left, expecting to see one of the musclemen, but instead, she made contact with Wade's muscled back in her face. He completely stepped in front of her, pushing her behind his wide frame as if she needed his protection. She may be small, but she could hold her own.

Lacey shifted to Wade's right to see who shouted at them to stop. One look, and she saw a security guard headed their way. But one glance from Wade, and she knew he was about to blow his top.

"Get back behind me until I know it's safe," he said through clenched teeth.

"Just because I'm Jeff's little sister, you don't have to protect me. I'm tough, and he taught me everything I need to know to ward off danger."

"This isn't your little racetrack. The moment you left home to come see me, you put yourself on a much more dangerous course. One that puts me in a position to protect you. Now get behind me." His blues blazed like ice.

Lacey slunk back behind him as the guard stepped up. "That dog can't be in here."

"She's a service animal," Wade replied, his voice monotone. "Where I go, she goes."

"You don't look disabled to me," the guard said, and Lacey dropped her mouth in astonishment at the guy's callous remark.

With every second of being kept hidden, Lacey felt her blood boil. A look to her feet and she could see the toe of her boot tapping. The next second, Promise nudged her clenched fist and grabbed her attention. Slowly, Lacey released her fingers to dig them into the dog's soft golden-red fur. She watched her fuzzy eyebrows bounce, first one then the other. It reminded Lacey of a dancing caterpillar, and made her giggle. So quick, her anger simmered to a slow boil, then to nothing. There was just no getting angry around this animal. Promise offered so much love and made a person redirect their negativity into a positive response to return her love back to her.

"No, I don't suppose I do," Wade replied to the guard. He reached into his back blue-jeans pocket under his army coat and removed his wallet. Lacey could hear him flap out a folded piece of paper she could only assume he handed over to the guard to read.

Lacey thought he would say more about his PTSD injury, but he didn't.

"We're very strict about animals on the trains. Service animals only," the guard said.

"As you can see by the document, she's certified."

That was all Wade planned to say? Lacey risked a glance from behind the patch on his upper right arm. The guard pored over the paper, obviously hoping for some falsification. She couldn't stand here and allow this unfairness to go on. She had to speak her mind.

"This man is a captain in the US Army. He fought for you to keep your freedom. He has a right to have this dog to help him now."

"Lacey," Wade warned. "Not every battle is worth the fight."

"Promise is worth it. And so are—" She stopped abruptly. The false words of affirmation stuck on her tongue. However indirectly, this man was responsible for her brother's death.

"Not to worry. I know I'm not worth it."

The guard handed the paper back. "Where's the dog's vest and leash?"

Wade reached into one of the many pockets of his

coat and traded the paper for something red. "I have the vest here, but we had to leave in a hurry and the leash was forgotten."

An excruciating amount of discretion time punctuated the conversation. Finally the guard said, "The dog should be on a leash…but since it's Christmas, I'll let it go. Just put the vest on her."

Wade snapped the red service cape to Promise's collar, then grabbed Lacey's arm to move her forward, but the guard halted them again with "Hey, buddy."

Wade turned back. "Yes?"

"Just so you know, I am thankful for your service." The guard nodded and went back to his post.

Wade didn't wait for any more interruptions. "We've got to move," he said, hustling her forward.

He led the way down some stairs to a row of lockers against a wall. After a quick look around the near-empty station, he put out his hand for the key.

Lacey lifted it over her head and gave it to him. Locker number 726 accepted the key, and a quick turn later, the metal door swung wide with a creak and clatter.

"Any particular reason why you chose 726?" Lacey asked as Wade reached in for the sole contents.

Another envelope.

"It's the month and date of the accident."

"*Your* accident? The one that left you an orphan and your sister burned and your baby brother dead?"

His mouth dropped at all the information she already knew. "July 26. At 4:20 p.m., if you want all the details, *Questions*."

"So you were investigating your accident and asked Jeff to help. Is he the one who told you your mother was a spy?"

"Shh." He scanned around them and whispered, "No. I

figured that out when I was eighteen. I found some information that told me my mom was not the person I thought she was. I found a collection of her aliases in one of her secret rooms. It was her Russian identities that had me leaving for the army the next day, needing to get away. But then one day I had this need to know what happened, who she really was. I thought if I did some investigating, it might make the images go away."

"What kind of images?"

"Images you won't understand, and shouldn't. Anyway, that's how I met your brother. He caught me snooping. When I told him why, he said he might be able to help. We set this locker up as a place to pass information without anyone knowing. Or thought we had anyway."

Wade read the name written on the envelope. He lifted his head and showed it to her. "Except this is to you. Not me."

"Me? But how would I know to come here for it? He left me the key and a piece of paper with your name on it. But there were no directions for the locker. If I hadn't gone to find you, I wouldn't have ever known it was here."

"Acting first must be a pattern of yours he knows well."

Lacey snatched the envelope. "So what? I'm driven. Some would say that's a good quality to have."

"If you have a death wish, sure."

Lacey barely heard his remark because seeing her name scrawled on the front of the envelope written in Jeff's handwriting nearly undid her. Tears sprang to her eyes as she realized this was the last letter Jeff wrote to her and would ever write again.

"Would you mind if I read this in private?" She looked at Wade over the paper, the feeling of moisture in her eyes.

Wade gave a quick nod. "I'll be over by the stairs.

Don't take too long." Promise followed her soldier, and as soon as Lacey heard the tap of his boots and the click of Promise's claws fade away, she ripped open the envelope and withdrew the single-page letter.

The first words brought more tears to her eyes and clouded her vision so much she could barely read on. Her hands shook as Jeff stated that if she was reading this then he was dead. But nothing could stop her from reading on, not her tears and not the goons out there hunting her.

His words lectured her on getting along with Mama, but also told her to stay strong, and to remember everything he taught her. She wasn't one of those dainty pieces of lace, he reminded her for the millionth time in her life. Lacey smiled at the words of her champion. What would she do without him cheering her on?

She exhaled and glanced at Wade, who was getting antsy by the stairs. Promise pushed against his thigh.

Lacey went back to the letter and read a part meant for him. Jeff wanted Wade to know he didn't regret a thing. She read on, then dropped the letter to her side when the words ended too soon. Her brother signed off with a message for Wade to go home and to always remember words were powerful. Whatever that meant. Maybe something to do with his healing, Lacey thought. It would make sense that Jeffrey would encourage Wade to talk about his pain. The man seemed to keep everything in, especially whatever those images were that he'd mentioned.

Lacey gazed down at the bottom of the letter. A long line of numbers was scrawled there, but she had no idea what they meant, either.

"What does it say?" Wade caught her unaware. She hadn't even heard his footsteps return.

Lacey held out the letter and held her breath as he read. He wasn't going to like what Jeff had to say to him. After a minute of his own perusal, he looked back at her, befuddled.

"He wants me to go home and give up? I don't believe it. We were getting so close."

"And he got too close. Jeff obviously doesn't want the same thing to happen to you." She pointed to the letter. "What are those numbers at the bottom of the page? I don't understand them."

"They're coordinates." Wade handed the letter to her while he pushed some buttons on his watch. "Huh."

"What? What did you do to your watch?" She stuffed the letter into Clay's interior suit-coat pocket.

"I input the numbers to get the location." He turned his wrist to show her the address that came up. "It's my family's racetrack."

"Maybe it was Jeff's way of telling you this was your home."

Wade shook his head. "It's best if I stay away from there."

"Why?"

"You won't get it."

"Try me."

Wade sighed and looked ready to bolt. This question affected him. Just when she thought he would take off, he surprised her and said, "I'm not whole, and that's all I'm going to say. Now let's get out of here."

"Back to New Hampshire?"

"Back to square one."

They retraced their steps in silence and exited the station with caution.

"It's too quiet," Wade whispered more to himself. "We should have heard or seen someone by now."

"You sound disappointed."

"I like being in control of the situation."

They reached the halfway point to the car when Wade put an arm out to halt her and Promise. "The tires are flat. It's a setup. Get back in the station now."

Lacey and Promise turned tail on a dime and followed his orders. Wade went right up to the teller. He bought two tickets for the next train leaving the station in two minutes—going south.

"You better hurry or you won't make it to the platform in time," the teller said as he passed the tickets through the glass opening.

Wade didn't wait for his change or to reply, but rushed them all through the station and out to the correct track.

The train waited on the empty platform; its doors would close on them any second. Lacey's breath panted loudly in her ears. All their steps hit the walk like a stampede, but it was Wade who rushed ahead and made it to the door. He stopped it from closing with his hand. With all his might, he pushed it wide with one hand while he reached for Lacey with his other.

"Hurry!" he shouted. Quickly, his gaze went past her shoulder, his eyes narrowed and darkened. "Lacey! Run!"

Just then, Lacey felt a strong, beefy hand cover her mouth and yank her back into a hard chest, her feet dangling above the concrete. With her eyes on Wade, she never saw him coming. She'd been completely blindsided.

Lacey couldn't see the man, but she could see Wade—and the look of conflict that washed over his face. He had two choices. Let go of the door, or let go of her.

She would tell him to hang on to the door if she could. She figured she would get out of the hold in just a second. A race-car driver had to be in top body shape to handle the strength of the cars and crashes. In the past, she'd climbed out of wrecked vehicles that were more constricted than this guy's arms. But struggling in his grasp now did nothing to loosen his hold or stop him from dragging her back into his hiding spot, out from everyone's view. She screeched from behind his sweaty hand, ignoring the awful salty taste and searching for a glimpse of Wade. She could no longer see him on the other side of a support beam. Her screeching was cut off when the guy moved his arm down to a choke hold. With his forearm at her throat, the only sounds she heard were the gurgles of the last of her air.

She thought of Promise. Did the dog know how to attack? Lacey had only seen the service animal offer tender care. Perhaps if it was Wade who needed the assistance, Promise would bare her teeth, but Lacey wasn't her handler. And since the dog was trained not to leave her handler's side, Lacey couldn't depend on the dog to help her.

"Give me what was in the box, and I'll make this quick and painless," the gruff voice spoke in her ear.

Lacey forced her mind to think clearly. Panicking now would only get her killed. How many times had Jeff told her that? She pulled from Jeff's training to help her out of this situation. Her army brother had instructed her not only on the track, but also in the gym. Getting out of a choke hold had been covered on the first day. Jeff had spent hours grabbing her from behind, calling her names like Frills and Ruffles. He'd really known how to make her head steam.

Lacey pictured her taunting brother and used her anger to push the beefy arm up and out. The break of the hold allowed her to turn toward the man and take his arm with her. She twisted it behind him and kicked the back of his leg just as the train's whistle blew. He let out a scream of pain as she brought him to his knees and elbowed his nose straight back into his head. Not a person heard him over the train, but she heard her brother's praises as though he called to her from the side of the mat. She would have loved to reminisce longer over the memories, but the train was leaving.

The green flag in Lacey's mind's eye waved. This was no time for a pit stop. She had to scram or be left behind. She hated being left behind.

She stepped around the brick wall and found the train car door closed and Wade and Promise gone.

It appeared Wade had made his decision.

He'd decided to let her go.

FOUR

The day had just begun, and he'd already lost the girl. What was Jeff thinking sending his sister north? Wade wondered, but he couldn't spend a second speculating his friend's motive. Not if he meant to make sure she stayed alive.

He inched stealthily around the opposing side of the brick partition that Lacey had been dragged off to moments before. He hoped to intercept her kidnapper from the other side and put an end to this ambush before she was taken off the platform to an unknown destination.

Wade went for his gun at the back of his waistband, then remembered he'd taken it out at Roni's request back at the house. He gave a slight growl. Hand to hand it would have to be. But that meant making sure the other guy was empty-handed, too.

Wade backed up against the wall to peer around the corner. Nothing and nobody. Not the kidnapper or Lacey. He nearly returned to the other side of the wall to see if they'd come back out that way. Then he saw the man in black—hunched over on the ground.

Lacey Phillips escaped from her captor all on her own?

Maybe her quick-witted motto did work for her after all, Wade thought as he stepped up to the guy she'd somehow put down. The thug was slowly gaining his feet and had his back to Wade.

Big mistake.

But apparently, it wasn't the assailant's first mistake of the day. Messing with Lacey Phillips took that slot.

The train behind the wall pealed its final whistle just as Wade latched on to the man's collar. He lifted and slammed him up against the bricks in one surprising swoop. "Who are you?" Wade held the man up by his black leather coat. He noticed the coat was snug on the pudgy guy. A lot of fast-food eating in between jobs would do that to you. "Who do you work for?" Wade demanded.

Spit flew from the criminal's lips as his answer.

Wade made no move, not even to swipe his face clean. The whistle ended, but its earsplitting noise was only replaced by repetitious banging—and a woman yelling.

Lacey.

"Let me on!" Her deep voice was unmistakable. "I won't let you leave me behind, Spencer! Do you hear me! Someone! Anyone! Let me on!"

The guy in Wade's hands cackled. "End of the line, Spencer," he said. Then he kicked out right into Wade's gut. With Wade's hands still gripped tight to the front of the thug's coat, all he had to do was give a quick pull forward. He snapped the man's head back hard against the brick wall.

Lights out.

The guy slumped back to the concrete platform where Lacey had left him before. He groaned as he fell forward, unconscious.

Wade raced around the wall and passed over to the other track. Lacey was pulling on the lever to the metal sliding door, but it wasn't budging for her.

"Let me try." Wade took hold of the handle.

She whipped around, shock on her face, her mouth dropped to a perfect oval. “I thought…”

“I know what you thought. A little something you should know about me. I don’t leave anyone behind. I had to do that once. I won’t do it again.”

“Your family. That’s who you left behind. You can’t blame yourself for that. You were eight years old.”

Wade shot a look into Lacey’s brown eyes that were just as piercing as her words. It appeared Questions had been poking her nose where it didn’t belong again. Wade gave the door a hard-and-fast shove wide, but quickly saw their path was not clear. A conductor with his navy blue cap blocked their way.

“Hey, you two! Is this your dog running through my train?”

“Yes!” Wade grabbed Promise from the man’s tight grip on her collar. He pushed his way in, pulling Lacey’s forearm behind him until they were both safe inside. “So sorry, sir. She took off and made it on board before we could. I’m so glad you found her. And that you didn’t depart without us.” Wade had made a good choice in commanding Promise to run down the aisle to give them a little more time.

“We didn’t have much choice, now, did we?” The man looked down through his round wire-framed glasses, his lips pinched beneath a thick brown mustache. “Can’t very well leave when there is an unleashed, unaccompanied canine roaming free in the aisles.”

“No, I guess you can’t.” The metal door slid home behind them. Wade nearly sagged against it in relief at having the door between them and the guy bent on killing one of them, or both.

But were there more? Wade doubted Pudgy worked alone.

"You two need to find your seats. You've already ruined my schedule for the day as it is."

"I'm sorry. Really, but you wouldn't happen to know if some interesting characters boarded the train right before us, would you?"

The whistle blew and the train jerked forward. Lacey shot a hand out for the closest thing to brace herself.

Him.

She quickly retracted for the wall instead. He still wasn't her favorite person.

But then, that wasn't his mission.

Wade gave his attention to the conductor. "Can you just tell us, sir, if some men in sunglasses and dressed in black boarded before us?"

"It's been a slow Christmas morning. I can count the travelers on two hands. And none of them fit that description."

Now Wade really wanted to sigh with relief. They'd been given a reprieve to strategize their next move. "How long until the next stop?"

"Seventeen minutes exactly." The conductor moved on to the next car to start clicking tickets.

Wade stepped into the car and studied the blur of trees as the train sped by, faster and faster. Out there were a couple of thugs racing them to the next train stop seventeen minutes away. He had to figure out a way to keep them from boarding. "Tell me, Lace, how are you with racing against a clock?"

"It's Lacey, and a clock doesn't scare me."

"Yeah, well, this clock has a killer, or two, waiting for you at the end. A little fear just might keep you alive."

After ten stops and still no sign of her pursuers, Lacey dropped her head against the glass window and watched the world go by at high speed. All day long she'd held her breath as the train pulled into each station or depot, then released her pent-up anxiety when Wade walked back through the car and gave the shake. Part of her just wanted to get this over and done with. The other part hoped they'd come far enough south to lose their pursuers completely.

Outside the window, the wintry barrenness of the north had gradually changed as the train took them into familiar territory. The terrain turned swampy as they chugged through South Carolina, with cypress trees drooping along the edges of the tracks. Lacey lifted her face to the not-so-far distance, knowing her home drew closer. But going home wasn't an option. She still had no answers, and now she had men following her. She wouldn't lead them to her parents.

Promise whined from her spot on the floor. She lifted her head from her paw. That only meant one thing.

Wade was passing by again.

The man had barely sat with them all day. When he did, it was brief, and when his legs began to bounce, he was up and walking again.

Promise pushed to all fours, and then sat in her typical ready-to-serve position.

"Your dog is amazing," Lacey said, aware that Wade was coming down the aisle from behind. "She knows everything about you, including knowing wherever you are."

"She was well trained." He stopped at their seats but didn't take one. Instead, Wade watched the window, then the two doors at each end of the car, then the two other passengers sitting in the car...again.

The man was in full ops mode.

Promise whined as she looked at her handler. Wade gave her a quick pat.

"I'm all right, Promise." He scratched the dog's head between her floppy ears. "Just working."

"She senses you're stressed. Is that why she's been whining?"

"Something like that."

"Something like that but not really. Is that what you're struggling to say?"

"I wasn't struggling. I just wasn't sharing."

"Right, because you don't share. Ever."

"The last person I shared with is dead." Wade looked at the other passengers then lowered his voice. "In case you've forgotten what happened to your brother."

"No, I haven't forgotten. I can't ever forget that, and I also won't forget you had a part to play in it, either. You will start sharing, whether you like it or not."

"It's not about me liking it. It's about keeping you alive."

"I'm not in any danger at the moment. We're on a moving train with no bad guys onboard. So why don't you have a seat and get comfy."

"I can't. I need to plan."

"Plan for what? You can't plan for anything if you don't know the variables. And even then, all your plans could be for nothing."

"All right, so why don't you tell me what you would do if two guys boarded right now and came through that door with the sole intent of taking you out."

"It wouldn't be the first time someone tried to take me out. Take me out of the race, take me off the track. The road kind or this one. It's all the same. It's always a battle of wits."

"What would you do? That's all I asked. If you're so quick-witted, tell me."

"Don't you get it? I can't tell you. That would be *planning*. I wouldn't know what I would do until I was in the moment. When I saw where my assailant came at me, from what direction, with what kind of weapon. When I'm driving, I have to have eyes all around me. A wreck up ahead needs to be avoided. A bully pushing me out of the race needs to be pushed back." Lacey shook her head in disbelief. "You own a racetrack. Do you know anything about racing at all?"

"I let Clay and Roni handle the business. I wish my name wasn't tied to the place at all."

"Seriously? I didn't get to see it when I was at your house, but I've heard it's a beautiful road track. Even drivers who prefer the oval have said a ride on Spencer Speedway is like a race through God's creation, the way the track follows the natural landscape of the New Hampshire byways. Have you ever driven it at all?"

"Not since I was a kid."

"You haven't been on your family's track since you were a child? Do you mean before the accident even?"

"So what?"

"So maybe you should try it. Not to race. Just to take one of your beautiful vintage cars out for a joyride with no one else on the track. Just you and the car. It might help you—"

"Stop. You sound like Roni. If I won't listen to her, why would I listen to you?"

Lacey pursed her lips. "Because *I* don't have any reason to help you. In fact, I don't care about you one bit. I don't even like you. I'm surprised your dog likes you."

Wade's lips twitched. "She doesn't. She's trained to

provide a service and duty to me. That's what you see. That's all."

"If that's what you believe, then you are blind, Wade Spencer." Lacey leaned over and petted Promise's satiny coat down her back. "This dog adores you. I see it the way she looks at you. She's so attentive."

Wade grew quiet. Lacey figured he'd returned to his pacing and planning. Then he appeared in front of her and took the seat opposite hers. She turned to look out the window to escape his silent scrutiny and pretended to be interested in the world flying by. After relentless seconds, she couldn't take it anymore.

"What?" she demanded.

"Where did you learn to escape the hold that guy back there had on you?"

Lacey gazed back out the window, remembering. "Jeff taught me. He taught me a lot."

"Because he was planning ahead."

"No. He couldn't have ever known I would be in that situation. It's not something you can plan for. All you can do is be ready if it ever happens."

"Which it did. When did he teach you?"

"Why does it matter?"

"Your brother was methodical. Nothing got past him. He had to have known you would need these skills."

"You're paranoid. Race-car drivers have to be in prime shape. Every muscle in our bodies works to control a heavy moving vehicle traveling at high speeds. If we lose it, especially around those turns, we're done for. It requires strength and stamina."

"And self-defense? Who's going to jump you while you're driving? Or is the paddock really that filled with unsavory characters that your brother thought it necessary to teach you escape tactics?"

Lacey leaned back in her seat. She crossed her arms at her front. "Why does it sound as if you're unhappy that I got away from the fat goon? Or are you just jealous because I did it without your help? Can't handle a woman who can take care of herself?"

"Just answer the question. When did he start training you in self-defense?"

Lacey swallowed hard, hesitating because what if Wade was onto something? What if Jeff had known she would need these skills? What if he had been planning ahead without her knowledge of it?

"Lacey—"

"All right! Fine." She sat forward. "Eight months ago on his last leave. He set me up with a trainer and made me continue even after he was gone."

"And you did?"

"Of course. I did everything Jeff told me to do. He's been in my corner my whole life. Or…*was*. Even now that he's gone, I…"

"Go on."

"I still hear him in my head. I still hear all the directions and insight he gave me." Lacey felt her lips tremble and she pressed them tight. She dropped her gaze to her hands in her lap. "The truth is—when I said I'm quick-witted, I meant Jeff was. I was just an attentive student. A kid sister who adored her bro—" Lacey scrunched her eyes closed and covered her mouth to stifle a cry. The raw pain cut through her chest fast and severe. Her breathing picked up as she worked through the sting and tried to gather her control.

Suddenly a paw touched her leg. The dog was a wonder at sensing a person's discomfort, even when the person wasn't her handler.

Lacey opened her eyes to pet Promise, but inhaled when she found the touch belonged to Wade.

He had leaned forward and placed the tips of his fingers on her knee. By the way his fingers fidgeted, he didn't look all too comfortable reaching out to her.

Lacey didn't say a word. She wasn't exactly comfortable with him touching her, either. And he wasn't welcome to. After all, she couldn't forget her brother was dead because of this man. Seconds turned into minutes as the world around her blurred into a haze of confusion and guilt. Guilt because she had yet to push him off.

What was wrong with her? She was supposed to hate this man, not want his comfort. Not latch on to the only person closer to Jeff than herself.

Lacey shot her head up, her attention given completely over to the man staring at her. That had to be it. Her impulse to keep him close was only because Jeff had called him a friend.

"You're my last connection to Jeffrey," she admitted quietly.

"I'm no substitute for your brother. He was a good man."

"The best."

Wade nodded. "But if he knew enough to start preparing you to defend yourself, then he must have known something was coming. Why didn't he tell me?"

"Maybe for the same reason he didn't tell me. We would tell him to stop. For his sake and for ours."

Suddenly, the train lurched and Lacey fell forward, nearly coming off her seat. If it wasn't for Wade's arms shooting out to catch her in his grasp, she would have flown over his seat. The train's brakes squealed in protest as it tried to bring all the cars to a stop.

"Hold on!" Wade yelled over the screeching noise. He

pushed her back against the momentum of the careening train. The muscles in his arms bulged under her fingers where they latched on to brace herself in the unsteady, out-of-control train car.

"Are we crashing? Or coming off the track? What's going on?" she pleaded.

"I don't know! Get down on the floor between the benches. Lie flat. I'll be right back!"

Wade left her crouched down with Promise as he went from one seat to the next, using the seat-back cushions for balance as the train still screamed to a stop. Lacey thought for sure the train was about to derail, if it hadn't already. Then she thought about what would happen if her car became disconnected and Wade wasn't in here when it did. They might be separated.

"Wade! Stop." She pushed to her knees to crawl out. "Don't leave me!" The words came out sounding so pathetic that on any other day she would have berated herself.

On her knees, she reached the aisle to see Wade at the door. He looked back at her. "Stay with Promise. I'll be right back."

The metal door slid open, and Wade stepped into the next car, letting it slam shut behind him.

The train trembled beneath her and knocked her to the floor. Lacey wondered what would happen when she finally came to a stop—and who would be waiting for her when she did.

"Stay? I don't think so." Lacey got to her knees. "Come on, Promise. Let's get out of here."

FIVE

The train came to a screeching stop. Wade hit the floor on full impact. His face felt the burn of the carpet as he slid a few more feet from the momentum.

Wade jumped to his feet to reach the front car, the destination he had been heading for before he went airborne. The conductor met him in the aisle.

"Get back to your seat until you're told to evacuate."

"What's going on?" Wade ignored the directions. "Did the train hit something?"

"A car was stuck on the tracks. It's safer for everyone to stay seated while emergency personnel are called in to assess the damage."

"And casualties, I'm assuming."

"I can only assume, too."

"I can help. I'm military. Four tours overseas. I've seen everything. Explosions, gunshots, fire…death." Wade swallowed the lump that image evoked. It didn't matter how old the traumas were. They were always fresh in his mind.

"Good to know. Go sit in your seat so I know where to find you. Let everyone in the last two cars know to wait for instructions."

Wade followed the conductor on his heels until he

reached the next car. The man opened the exit door and jumped down a good three feet, landing in a run back where the train had come from. Wade held the support bar and leaned out to see if he could find the wreckage. The color red sprinkled the tracks and surrounding swampland, car parts or what was left of them.

"Get back in the train!" the conductor yelled back over his shoulder when he noticed Wade hadn't followed his directions.

The color of the car pieces pulled his attention. A distinct cherry red that had him asking, "What kind of car was it?"

"The engineer said it was a Ferrari. Now get back inside!"

Wade gave a quick scan into the dense trees and surrounding swamps that spread for miles and miles in this part of South Carolina. But it wasn't the cypress trees he was looking at. It was who might be lurking in them, waiting for him and Lacey to disembark.

Or using this ample time to board while no one noticed. In fact, they could already be on board. They could already have found her sitting alone and unprotected because he left her behind—after he'd told he would never do that again.

Wade whipped through one empty car then the next. He raced down the aisle and burst through to the next and finally his and Lacey's car.

Empty.

He took a few steps toward the dining car in the rear but stopped when the door on the other end slid open. Wade halted his steps.

Two men dressed in black stepped in, reaching for something inside their coats at the same time. Wade stepped back and hit the button to slide his door open. He dropped to the floor, knowing a bullet would be coming for him. The door slammed shut on his foot just as two thuds hit the door. Bullets meant for him lodged in the bulletproof glass above. Wade yanked his foot through to let the door slam shut completely.

Two doors stood before him from this vestibule between cars. One led to the next car and one led outside. Wade had less than a second to decide which one to take. He wondered what quick-witted Lacey would do in this split-second decision as he did what he'd already planned to do earlier.

Go up.

But not before he made sure the two goons saw him. If he could lead them away, Lacey—wherever she was—would be safe.

Lacey absently rustled her hand through Promise's fur from their spot on the floor of the bathroom. She'd jumped in here and locked the door when the train had finally come to a stop. She figured she would be safe until she knew what was going on. "Do you think they're out there?" Lacey whispered to Promise. "I can only assume the musclemen have caught up to me again."

A knock came on the door, causing Promise to stand to the ready. "Is someone in there?" A woman's voice was heard.

"Taken." Lacey disguised her voice to that of a gruff old man, not too hard to do, since she always believed she sounded like a man with her deep voice anyway.

"In case you didn't know, the train hit a car left on the track. I heard it was a Ferrari."

"A Ferrari!" So much for her deep voice. She thought she actually shrieked like a girl just then. She altered her voice again to ask, "Who would leave a Ferrari on the track?" *As if she didn't know.* It had to be the same Ferrari she and Wade drove down in last night. What better way for these losers to stop the train than to use Wade's own car.

But that only meant one thing: the losers were out there.

Lacey reached into Clay's suit coat pocket for the envelope. She should just give it to them. For some reason, they were willing to kill her for it. She couldn't see why. It was just a goodbye letter from a brother to his sister.

Lacey folded it in thirds and stuffed it into her jeans front pocket. These were Jeffrey's last words to her. She wouldn't be giving them up.

When outside noises ceased, she took the chance and peeked out the door. A quick scan showed the car empty. The few passengers that had been in there when she'd entered earlier had left, either for another car or for a closer look at the scene outside.

How could they even look at such a heart-wrenching scene? She didn't want to imagine the Ferrari mangled beyond recognition.

She headed toward the front of the train, wondering where Wade was. Did he need Promise? He should have taken his dog with him.

Lacey stepped out of the car and into the open area between the car and the engine. All was quiet inside. It would appear even the engineer had gone to inspect the crash, as well.

A thud came from above and both Lacey and Promise looked up. Someone was on top of the train. Another thud came from farther down. Two somebodys were up there, she surmised.

Was one of them Wade?

Lacey pushed the exit door wide and looked out. Immediately she stepped back inside. A ten-foot drop met her beyond the train's step. There was no way she could leave this way, or risk a broken neck as she tumbled down into a wet marsh filled with a myriad of organisms that called it their home.

Lacey hit the button to open the interior door, but the door on the opposite end also opened. The guy who'd grabbed her back at the station entered. The very same man she'd left on the ground holding his nose. Judging by the snarl on his face as he stared her down from across the car, he looked ripe for revenge.

Lacey hit the button and let her door slide closed. The ten-foot drop it would be.

Wade's body lifted off the steel rooftop of the train, nothing but air beneath him, his head snapping back from the blow just dealt to him. With nothing to grab hold of to brace his fall, he landed on his back with a bone-cracking thud against unrelenting, slippery steel. His body continued to progress at high speed right to the edge.

Wade's head screamed in agony, but he still had enough sense to lock the heels of his boots into a crevice in the roof. His body jerked to a stop while his head rang louder than the police sirens off in the distance. Help was coming, but they weren't here yet. Wade lifted his head before the guy got a second shot off, but his vision clouded and blurred. A search for his assailant through blinking eyes only made the world tip one way then the next. Wade rolled to his right, nearly falling off the edge. He held himself steady but caught a blurry glimpse of Lacey and Promise in the swampy water below.

Had they jumped from the train?

That could only mean one thing.

Wade scanned the ground below just as the other guy

ran by. Pudgy had exited the train where the ground wasn't so steep and wet. Still, he would be on Lacey in seconds. Long before the police arrived to stop him.

Wade pushed up to go after him, but before he could make a move, the unmistakable barrel of a gun jammed into his back.

"Not so fast," the guy behind him said. "This is how it's going to go. You're going to climb down the ladder and follow the girl into the woods, and you're going to do it quietly."

The woods? Wade shot a look to the swamp, now empty. Across the way, he saw Lacey and Promise disappearing into the trees. The woods were the worst place she could be going. Didn't she hear the sirens getting closer? *No, Lacey*, Wade pleaded silently. She was going the wrong way. What kind of split-second decision did she call that?

"Try anything and I'll kill you first. Then, you'll be of no help to her at all."

Wade swallowed hard. The guy was right. Wade's only choice was to do as he was told, for now, especially since Pudgy was gaining on Lacey fast.

With each step down the rungs, then into the woods, Wade planned his next moves. Get to Pudgy before Pudgy got to Lacey was number one—and before the gun wielder decided they were far enough from people to dispose of him.

Just before entering the thick tree line, Wade saw the conductor appear around the far end of the train. The gun pushed harder, the message loud and clear. The conductor climbed aboard the last car without notice of them at this end. When would he notice two of his passengers were unaccounted for? Would there be a search for them?

Wade's boots hit water. Splashes hit his knees as the swampy land became more saturated and deeper.

Wade pretended to trip, dropping to his knees in the water with a loud splash.

"Get up!" the gunman said.

"Sorry. I tripped on a root or something," Wade mumbled as he pushed up and swung around, sweeping his arm through the murky water as he turned. As hoped, the water hit the guy smack in the eyes, long enough for Wade to make a grab for the gun.

But the guy held tight and swung his arm off to his right to break Wade's hold. The quick action and slippery water caused Wade to lose his grip, but it also caused the guy to lose his.

The gun flew from his hand, landing in the thick, dark water with a gulp. For a split second the guy looked to the sludge in shock and distaste.

A split second was all Wade needed. He reached for the left arm pocket of his combat jacket and withdrew a small pocketknife. Before the guy turned back, the knife was flipped open to flash a warning. A few quick slices produced tears in the goon's black leather coat in case he didn't heed the warning. The momentum had him falling back, arms flailing wildly, and Wade took off in the direction Lacey went before the man hit the water.

Wade's high-speed run splashed through the swamp, but he could still hear the guy sputtering obscenities and lethal promises. If Lacey wasn't under pursuit, Wade would have stuck around to use the water as a way to get information out of the thug's lips instead of his useless lewd comments.

Another day.

With the knife in his palm, Wade went in search of Pudgy. The guy had to be stopped before he caught up with Lacey, but the setting sun outside the swamp was just a memory under the canopy of trees. Darkness loomed and grew with each sloshing step farther into the unknown terrain.

Again, in this dense myriad of tangled tree trunks and creeping branches, Wade wondered what Lacey had been thinking coming into this cold, dark place. Getting lost in here could mean death by natural causes by morning, never mind the paid assassins hunting them down. Wade couldn't wait to hear her quick-witted reason for leading them to their deaths.

Of course, that would mean he found her in here first.

And found her alive.

SIX

"I know you're around here! You might as well come out, missy. You can't hide. I will find you," Lacey's chaser called out through the swamp. She dared not moan from the pain in her wounded arm, or even breathe from her hiding place in fear of alerting him to the fact that she was much closer than he realized.

Like right above him.

From her perch on a thick branch, Lacey leaned closer to the trunk of the cypress she'd crawled up into. Promise stayed low and silent beside her. The man who called out was the same man from the train station. He trembled from cold where he stood in the knee-deep water, and from her bird's-eye view, he didn't look so scary now.

She knew that wasn't the truth, though. He had a duty, and it wasn't to be her friend.

His duty was to make her disappear.

This brute didn't get to where he was in his life by making friends. How many people had he killed with his stout hands? Hands she knew so up close and personal. The memory of his sweaty palms on her lips made her cringe.

He tunneled one of those killing hands through his

greasy black hair, a nervous gesture that made her think perhaps the trembling was from more than cold water.

Perhaps the man was afraid of failing at his duty.

That only told Lacey she had more to fear than *this* guy. If he caught her, she would be facing his boss next, and that made a tremor zip straight up her own spine.

A wet paw covered her hand on the branch.

Promise stared up at her with nervous, droopy eyes. She looked petrified in the darkness, but Lacey didn't know what to do to change that. They'd run for a while before she realized they were running in circles and would be safer up here. The guy's voice had died down for a little while, enough time to allow them to climb higher and higher before he came back around.

Lacey wished Promise had gone back to Wade. Instead, the dog had jumped up on the low webs of tangled cypress branches to stay by Lacey's side. With the sun gone and the lurking shadows to hide in, she felt safe, for now. She feared Promise would whine and give them away, but the control this dog had over her emotions so far said otherwise. It reminded Lacey of Wade's statement. *She's trained to provide a service.*

Just like the man below.

But Promise's duty was for something so much more heroic.

Lacey leaned over and saw the burly man had moved on in another direction. She buried her numb fingers into Promise's thick wet fur and whispered, "Why didn't you stay behind? You didn't need to jump out after me, you silly dog. I'm not your handler. I'm not the one you love and protect. And I know you love him. I see it, even if he doesn't."

Promise hedged in closer, pushing her head into Lacey's thigh. Her collar brushed against Lacey's hand when she petted her neck. Her red service vest attached to the collar was soaked and cold. Lacey thought of removing it, but before she could, water swished off in the distance, silencing all movements by them in the tree.

The guy was circling back again. Would he find her this time? Would he shoot her out of the tree? She plastered her back to the trunk, hoping her silhouette from below looked like any of the other distorted trees.

Even though Promise knew whining wasn't allowed, shivering couldn't be controlled—by either of them. The cold swamp water that drenched them seeped into their bones, chilling them more and more with the evening chill. Lacey did her best to control her teeth chattering.

The swishing of water grew louder. At any second she could be found. Did they just want her dead? Or were they after something more?

The guy said he wanted whatever was in the locker. Lacey felt her soaked jeans where the folded envelope was stuffed. It would be ruined by now. Would the words on the paper even be legible anymore? The message was useless to them when it was dry, and now it would be more so. Did that mean they would just kill her? Or would they take her to their leader? What would they do when they learned *she* was useless, as well?

The water below swashed louder and Lacey covered her mouth to stifle her breathing that sounded so loud in her ears. It wouldn't be long before all her questions had answers, unfortunately.

Her pursuer was so close now. The tinkling of water settled where he stopped on the other side of the tree below. She dared not move to look. Instead, Lacey braced herself to make a jump for it. She hoped she wouldn't have to, that the guy would think no one was in the area and turn around and leave again. And for good this time.

Please, God, cover us with Your protection. Let no one hear us, so they move away from here and leave us alone. But if I have to go, I know You'll go with me, Lord. I'm ready.

Lacey nodded in agreement with her prayer at the same time her fingers gripped into the bark of the tree. She was poised and ready to take the leap as soon as she caught one glimpse of the man.

But before Lacey made a move, Promise jumped up from her spot on the branch and dived down into the water with a splash, their location now revealed.

Lacey pushed herself harder back into the tree, panic setting in with the coming of faster breaths. She might as well give up, too. The race was finished. *Why, Promise? Why?*

Then she heard a familiar voice.

"Lacey, it's me, Wade. Come down quietly."

In less than a second, Lacey followed Promise's splashing leap.

So much for quiet.

Lacey plowed into the water at full force. Her legs barely hit bottom before his arms secured her and pulled her into his chest. She came down so hard they nearly fell back into the water. He stepped to a gnarled, silhouetted tree trunk for support.

"Lacey, you're safe, but you have to be still, or they'll hear you and come back."

As he hoped, she froze in his arms. But only for a second. She reached her arms up around his neck and pushed her face into its curve to stifle a soft whimper. He couldn't fault her for being afraid. His own fear matched hers.

Wade pushed his face into her matted hair as he felt

his heartbeat pulse through his skull. He squeezed tighter when his hands shook. Promise whined beside him. She sensed his tension, but Wade wasn't ready to let Lacey go.

And she wasn't ready, either.

"I shouldn't have left you," he said. "I should have—"

"No, you shouldn't have." Lacey clung on even though her words were accusative. "But you made the best decision you could have in the moment. There was no time to sit down and discuss things, draw up plans and delegate. A moment like that calls for action. It's fight or flight. But you should know, I don't run from anything and you don't have to leave me behind."

"Well, I can't leave you behind in these swamps, that's for sure, but we do need to fly. Those guys will be back. Why on earth did you choose to come in here? The police were on their way."

"I thought I could beat them on my turf. The swamps were my playground. Besides, the only reason you found me is because Promise gave us away."

Wade smirked in the darkness. She was right, but he wasn't about to admit it. He tipped her chin up to glean her emotions, exemplified through her shadowed eyes. "No fear of snakes, huh?"

"Just the pudgy kind."

Wade sobered and searched the perimeter around them for Pudgy and his friend. "We can't go back to the train. They'll block our path and catch us."

"Don't ask me for the way out of here. I'm directionally challenged. I've been going in circles for hours."

"You race cars. That's all you know how to do."

"Not the time for jokes, Wade. Now's the time for you to start all that planning you like to do."

Wade lifted his arm to show her his watch. "Judging by our current coordinates, I say we go left."

"Go left," Lacey repeated quietly.

"You don't agree?"

"It's not that. Go left was a command Jeffrey instructed me to do often. When you said it, it just reminded me of him."

Wade pulled Lacey's head down to his chest with a sigh. "I'm going to get you out of here, okay?"

She nodded, trembling.

Wade grabbed Lacey's upper arms and realized she only wore Cora's flowered blouse, now drenched.

"I lost your uncle's suit coat somewhere in the jump, I think," she answered as though she read his mind.

Wade took off his combat jacket and wrapped her up in it. He should have done that first thing, but all he could focus on was holding Lacey to make sure she was real, and he wasn't having one of his hallucinations.

Lacey pulled it closed on a sigh. "You should give this to Promise. She's been so wonderful."

"Don't worry, I'll take good care of her. That's my part in the deal. She guides and protects, I keep her happy and healthy." Wade hefted Promise up to situate her across his shoulders and back. She was drenched and frigid. He couldn't have her trouncing through the water anymore. He meant what he said. He didn't shirk on his duties to Promise. He couldn't. Without her, he'd be a puddle bigger than these swamps.

They took their first steps in the decided-upon direction. Water quietly splashed around their moving feet, taking them slowly away from the train and the dangerous men waiting for them to return to it.

After a good distance of silence, Wade spoke again. "I've never seen Promise protect anyone but me. She was trained, starting at three days old, to recognize human emotion, but she was only allowed to bond with me. Not that I'm not happy she stayed by your side—I am—but I am surprised."

"Maybe she was trained to sense danger in general. Not just danger for you, but for anyone."

"She was trained to be a guide dog for her handler—me."

Lacey shrugged as she followed beside him a couple steps. He noticed she became increasingly quieter as they moved through the swamp. In the darkness, he reached for her hand. Her fingers felt like frozen brittle sticks.

"Is everything all right?" he asked. "Besides being lost out in the swamps and chased by strangers who want to kill you, that is?"

She shrugged again. "I was thinking. I may have had something to do with us being separated back there, as well."

"How so?"

"You told me to stay down and I didn't. The thing is, I really do try to make the best choices in the moment. I guess this one wasn't that great."

Wade sighed. Could he really let her go on thinking she caused all this? No. He couldn't. "Actually, you getting out of that train car probably saved your life. The guys entered on your car and would have gotten to you before I did."

"Really?" Hope rushed into her voice. "See? What did I tell you? I'm quick-witted."

Wade felt a slow smile grow on his face. He was glad it was dark. He didn't need to encourage her further.

Wade lifted his watch to check their location, then pointed a finger for her to go right. "I think that's enough gloating for tonight. We're still lost in the swamps, if you didn't notice where your second choice led us."

"Figures you'd bring that up." She took the turn he

signaled, but it seemed extra water sprayed him when she did. Had Lacey just splashed him? He watched her turn her back on him, and this time he felt his smile grow even bigger. Bigger than any smile he ever remembered feeling on his face. He almost reached up to touch the new feeling.

Almost.

SEVEN

"I think they want the letter," Lacey said, her boots squishing with each step. They'd been on dry land for almost an hour, but still in the middle of nowhere in the pitch dark and cold. She shivered in her wet clothes. "There's got to be something in Jeff's message that we're not seeing." Lacey stopped when Wade made no reply. She walked alone. "Wade? Wade, where are you?"

"I'm over here," he called from her right. Lacey spun and faced more darkness. "I just wanted to make sure we weren't being followed."

"And?" She targeted her search in the direction his voice came until he stepped back into her vision and by her side again. Her fingers itched to reach for him.

"I think we're in the clear. For now. I see a cabin through the trees we can bunk in, but we better be gone by morning."

"Where?" All the mangled silhouettes of trees looked the same to her.

With a light touch of his palm on her cheek Wade directed her gaze straight ahead. His voice lowered as he spoke so close to her. "Even if those guys are lying low tonight because of the influx of police in the area due to the train, they'll be back out looking for us tomorrow."

His words should have heightened her fear, but his hand on her face, offering the same comfort as Promise's paw, calmed her instead. He had her frozen nerve endings thawing instantly and waking up. The heat he'd managed to hold on to through the swamps invited her to lean in and share. Lacey closed her eyes to relish the way her body stirred under his touch and forgot about the cold and evil for one blissful minute. She forgot about her defenses, as well. Weaknesses could be exploited by those closest to you, and Wade was getting mighty close.

"It looks as if it's unoccupied. I think it's all ours," he said, breaking the connection by dropping his arm.

Lacey covered where the cold night air stole away the warmth of Wade's touch, glad for the shroud of darkness that kept her vulnerability a secret.

"Come on, I'll race you," Wade said, oblivious to the way he'd just softened her.

Race? It took a second for Lacey to engage in the challenge, but she quickly ran ahead of him. Or maybe she ran from him.

Her hard shell was back in place when Promise came up alongside her, passing her like a pro. Lacey picked up her pace, but her frozen feet rendered her the loser in this one. Promise reached the wooden deck first and began a romping winner's-circle dance, her tongue hanging out in excitement.

Lacey dropped to her knees to pet the beautiful creature. "You're a good dog, Promise." Tears sprang to Lacey's eyes as she realized how faithful this dog had been to her today. "I wish I had a dog like you. I would love you so much."

"I never said I didn't love her." Wade stepped up behind them.

Lacey gained her feet. "No, I suppose you didn't. But rejecting her love is just as hurtful."

"Do you speak from experience?"

"I speak from witnessing relationships fall apart. Two of my friends who promised to love and cherish are already divorced. At least now they're not hurting each other anymore."

"Who says divorce is painless? There are some hurts that last a lifetime. I, too, have friends in the army who thought the pain would stop after divorce. It didn't." Wade and Promise left a silenced Lacey standing there as the two of them stepped up the deck steps, handler and companion, together again. Within minutes, Wade had the front door open and a lantern inside lit. "Are you coming?" he called out from somewhere in the house. "I know I said we should be safe, but you don't need to put my words to the test."

Lacey snapped to and set her legs in motion as she peered into the inky blackness of the forest around her. Anyone could be staring back at her and she wouldn't know it.

The cabin was cold, but the fireplace had to remain unlit. Too risky if the guys were close by. Lacey left the bedroom that would be hers for the night to find man and dog on the floor in the open area.

Wade finger-combed Promise's matted fur by lantern light and looked more relaxed than she'd seen him yet. Much more than when she met him in New Hampshire. "Does Roni know going home stresses you out?"

Wade shot a surprised look her way, then smirked. "Just what else did my uncle tell you?"

Lacey parked it on the braided rug beside him. "Sorry, your uncle might have mentioned something about your need for space. Not in a mean, gossipy way, though."

Wade looked to the flame. "Clay's like a father to me. He also understands me better than my sister does."

"Roni wants you to leave the military, doesn't she? So you can take on more responsibilities with the business?"

Wade nodded. "She also thinks I need to go home to heal."

"What's stopping you?"

He turned to look at her. "Back to Fifty Questions? Why do you want to know?"

Lacey shrugged and took up her turn to look into the light, away from his piercing eyes. "I guess I understand your sister's request. I asked Jeff to do the same, but for me it was…different."

"How so?"

She sighed and reached to pet Promise. "For me, it was purely selfish. You have to understand. I want to race cars, but with Jeff gone, I'm stuck in the shop. Don't get me wrong. I love working on the cars. But that's only because I know what's coming up on the weekend. The fruits of my labor. Except, without Jeffrey, I'm not working on my car. I'm working on somebody else's."

Promise moved in close to Wade with half her furry limbs over Wade's legs. She rested her head on his thigh.

Lacey gave a soft laugh at the sight. "She's so cute. And yet she's so strong and brave. You should have seen her today. I felt so protected with her by my side. She has the biggest heart I've ever seen. And she is so unselfish with it. She puts me to shame. I want to be Promise when I grow up."

"Oh, good, you plan on growing up. There's hope for you after all."

"Ha-ha, very funny. I'm laying my soul bare, and you're cracking jokes."

"Who's laughing?" He made a straight face, but his

dimple deepened. He was holding back a smile, whether he wanted to admit it or not.

"Not you, that's for sure. I don't think you know how to laugh."

His face darkened at her remark; his dimple turned rigid. He leaned in and reached for her wrist. He snatched it before she could pull away. With a quick flick of his fingers, he had the cuff of Cora's flowered blouse undone. He folded the sleeve up once, then twice. His stern gaze leveled on her while he worked. "FYI, Lacey. When one is used to putting bandages on people, they find it hard to laugh."

He made the last fold at her elbow and pushed the rest of the fabric up a little farther. There, her wet, mangled bandage barely stayed on. He undid the tape stuck to her skin. The bandage was soaked and useless, and honestly, she hadn't even thought to change it. Not that she had the means to do so.

Lacey watched him inspect her wound. He hovered close to her arm. Her forehead nearly bumped his cheek when she bent to try to see, as well.

He turned her arm toward the lantern light, cradling her elbow so gently in one of his hands. His gaze was as attentive as Promise's always was on him.

She cleared her throat, remembering Roni's scars, and who knew how many comrades he'd bandaged in war? "I guess I didn't think my remark through."

His blue eyes flashed up at her. "Can you repeat that?"

"Repeat what?"

"What you just said. About not thinking through something."

"Thinking through my remark. It was callous. I'm sorry. Who are you, my mother?"

He dropped her arm and pushed to his feet to stand

over her. Lacey raised her head to study his serious face. He turned away and walked to the kitchen to start opening cabinets and drawers.

The cabin was sparsely furnished with a few essentials. The standard place setting filled the cabinets. The place looked to be a rental. Wade bent over to look through a cabinet below, popping his head up when he slammed the door shut and walked back to her. He carried a white plastic box with a red cross stamped on the front cover.

"Another bandage?" she asked as he neared.

"Your wound needs to be cleaned or it'll be infected by tomorrow. The swamps didn't help it much."

"I can do it myself."

"With one hand? I'd like to see that."

Lacey had to concede. The next second he was back on the floor in front of her. His closeness felt stifling now. It had to be because of the way he saw her. She felt his judgment. She was tired of that feeling. She didn't measure up with her mother. She didn't measure up on the track. And apparently, she didn't measure up with Wade.

Why did she always feel as if she had to prove herself to people?

And why should she care when this was the man responsible for Jeff's death? She latched on to this fact. It was her strongest wall where this guy was concerned.

"This doesn't make up for your part in Jeff's death, you know."

Wade paused his ministrations to eye her again. "You're right. Nothing I can ever do will." He went back to swabbing. He placed a clean bandage over her wound again and broke the tape with his teeth. He rolled her sleeve back down, and the cold dampness of the fabric touched her where his warm hands had been. Lacey bit down to not let it bother her.

Wade went back to the kitchen, and the cabinets and drawers started sliding and banging again.

"Beef stew or chili?" he called over the island separating them. He placed two MREs on the counter. "Take your pick."

"Where'd you get those?"

"I keep them in my combat jacket."

"Of course you do. Always the planner."

"It's a good thing for you. Now, take your pick."

"Whatever you don't want," she answered, not really caring as long as it was food. Wade put two pots on the stovetop and within minutes the stew began to heat up.

He had his back to her while he divided their dinner into bowls; the scrape of the spoon against glass was the only sound in the cabin. Promise sat back on her haunches and watched Wade with her typical brown, liquid eyes, so full of attention just for him. A few minutes later, Wade turned back with three bowls. He handed over a beef stew to Lacey and another to Promise, before taking his seat by the lantern again.

Lacey picked up her spoon but her throat closed. She knew what she had to do before she could eat. She cleared her throat and pushed out a weak "Thank You, God, and…thank you, Wade."

"I know it's not a very fancy Christmas dinner. I wish it could be more."

Lacey lifted her head from her bowl to search for a clock. The one over the round kitchenette table said eleven forty-five. "It's still Christmas? I can't believe it. That feels like days ago."

"If you had known all this would transpire, would you have stayed home?"

Lacey brought the bowl to her lap and looked down into it. "No." She lifted her head to Wade. "My brother's dead. And I won't stop until I know why."

"You already know why. Because of me. I got him involved in trying to figure out who I am. It was my problem, not his."

Lacey sat back as a clearer picture formed. "This is more than finding out if your mother was a spy, isn't it? When you found *her* aliases at eighteen, you lost *your* identity."

Lacey's question lingered in the room as they ate. She thought of her own roots: Frank and Adelaide's daughter, born and raised in Mount Pleasant, South Carolina. Her parents' genealogy went beyond the Deep South to across the big pond. But these facts were all her heritage, not her identity.

Wade pushed to his feet and took the three finished bowls to the counter, his lips still sealed tight.

"Talk to me, Wade. We could be killed any second. Honesty is all we have left. Is your identity what you're looking for?"

With his back to her, he turned his head and said, "I've learned talking only gets people killed."

His leg bounced. He reached for his thigh with one hand. Promise moved into action and was at his side in the blink of an eye, looking for that hand to pet her. Lacey could only imagine how bad things would get without her attentiveness and skill.

Wade pet his dog for a few minutes. "You don't need to worry," he said.

"Worry?" She looked up from his petting hand and saw he watched her watching him.

"I see you looking at me. You're wondering if I'm

going to fall apart right here. Don't lie. You said honesty was all we had left."

Lacey gave a short nod. "All right. I did wonder what would happen without Promise here."

"I'd be on the floor curled up in a ball. My head would feel like it was about to explode, and I would be praying that it would. Then it would finally be over. All the images would be gone and couldn't remind me of what I've done."

Lacey went to the island where he stood. She took the tall stool. "What have you done?"

"I talked and got people killed." A sick laugh escaped his lips. He looked down at his dog. "Do you know why the army gave her to me?"

Lacey shrugged. "To help you deal with your injury."

"Sure. By *talking*. They want me to talk to her. They don't get it. I talk and people die. I talked when I was… eight." He swallowed and looked to the windows. With a shake of his hand he pushed Promise away and went to the door. Lacey thought he was about to leave and she jumped off the stool to stop him. But he stopped at the window, facing the door.

"What did you say? Who did you talk to?"

"Some guy at the track. You grew up climbing swamp trees. I grew up climbing the rungs of the grandstand at the track. It would drive my mother crazy. She was always telling me it wasn't a jungle gym, but every day I would try for a little higher before she caught me. Then one day I found something stashed between two of the joists. It was a black tube. A case of some kind. I brought it to my mom. She flipped out and told me not to tell anyone. Her response scared me, but not as much as when some guy grabbed me soon after and started shaking me, demanding to know where the spike went."

"What did you do?"

"I told him. I said, 'I gave it to my mom.' Just like that. I still hear myself saying it over and over to this day." Wade reached a hand to his forehead. "Why did I say anything at all? Now all I have is this image of her in my head. Her neck is…broken." His voice fell to a raw whisper at the end.

"What's a spike?" Lacey spoke to his back. Talking seemed to come easier for him when he wasn't facing her.

"A black capsule. About six inches by one inch. I was a kid. I had no idea what it was then. I know exactly what it is now. A dead-drop device spies passing intelligence will use. It's small and can fit into crevices or even the ground until the info can be retrieved. I may not have known what it was then, but my mother did. And four hours later we went over that ledge because I talked."

"Clay said it was an accident."

"Clay doesn't know what I found. I never told him. If I did, he would be dead, too."

"But you rescued your sister before—"

"Don't." Wade whipped around and captured her gaze. His darkened eyes glittered. His shaking arms crossed at his chest to keep away from Promise, who nudged him. He wanted no help or accolades from anyone. "Don't make me into some type of hero. I caused those burns on her, all because I opened my mouth. And the next time I opened it, your brother paid the price. Now you're next. If I can't fix this, you're dead. You can't make that pretty, so don't try."

Wade reached for the door. Before he stepped out on the deck, he said, "I'll keep watch tonight. Get some sleep, but be ready by five."

"Where are we going?"

"I'm taking you home."

Lacey inhaled. She would not be brought home like a little girl to her parents. But before she could protest, the door shut on her.

Lacey noticed Promise went with him, staying by his side. Even after he'd pushed her away, the dog continued to love him.

Lacey wanted to be angry with Wade, but instead she felt so sad that he was missing out on such pure and unconditional love. What would his life be like if he believed he was loved?

Lacey knew how she felt when she accepted Jesus' love. She'd found her identity and where she belonged, and it had nothing to do with her roots.

EIGHT

"Let us out at the corner," Wade said as he pulled out his wallet from his back pocket to pay the cabdriver.

Lacey put her hand on his arm. "But we still have another couple blocks to go before we reach my parents' house."

"We'll walk," he replied under his breath, ending the conversation until the driver pulled away. "We can't lead anyone to your parents' door."

Wade looked down the quiet main street of Lacey's pretty coastal town of Mount Pleasant. He could only hope he was making the right choice in bringing her back. He would hate for the danger to follow her here and to everyone she loved.

She scanned the other end of the block. "We should get off the street, then. Stay to the back of the yards and into the willows. Follow me."

They sneaked down the side of a house, then into the hanging covering of trees. They crossed over a brook on a few slick rocks. "Is this detour to get out of going home?" he asked.

"I'm not taking you to the house. I'm taking you to the shop. It's on the same property but out front. I want to make sure it's safe before I walk up to the front door and bring danger to my parents."

"Good thinking."

"Don't sound so surprised." She held back a few long twigs so Promise wouldn't get poked in the eyes.

Soon they were in the overgrowth of willow trees, shielded from view of the passing traffic on the street. The sound of engines was muffled from beneath the canopy even without the long branches sporting all their leaves. It gave the feeling of solitude and...concealment.

It dawned on Wade that his whole life felt as if he lived under the canopy of camouflage. One big cover-up. And he wasn't any closer to knowing the truth than when he'd found that capsule twenty-eight years ago. He wasn't any closer than when he found his mother's aliases when he was eighteen. He still knew nothing, and yet what little he did know got people killed.

He watched Lacey from the back as she led him forward. She'd tied up her long chocolaty hair in a mangled knot. Without a comb, it was the best she could manage. And yet she didn't voice a complaint about it. Roni would be squawking. With his own short military cut, a comb wasn't a concern, but it could have made the past twenty-four hours a little more bearable for Lacey. Maybe he'd get her one. *No.* He stopped that thought from taking root. She could comb her hair when she was home safe and sound.

And alive.

"How do you know these guys won't come after me in my own bed?" she called over her shoulder. "After you leave, I could still be in just as much danger."

"I'm calling the police before I leave to make sure they keep watch until things quiet down. Plus, I plan to make it look as if I brought you back to get rid of you. I want them to think that you don't know anything. That you're nothing but an annoying kid sister playing detective."

Lacey came to an abrupt halt, causing Wade to collide into her back. She whipped around, heat flaring in her brown eyes an inch from his. "*Playing* detective? I've never *played* at anything. I never played dress-up. I never played with dolls. I don't hide behind fantasy and make-believe. That's my mother's department with all the weddings she stages. They're nothing but a veil covering up the truth of marriage. I face things head-on, with no blinders."

"The truth of marriage? And what's that, you who have never been married?"

"That it's hard. That it's not all flowers and sugar, smiles and lace. Love isn't shown in speeches. It's shown in actions and in truth and sticking by each other when things are difficult. The truth is, this person you are vowing to love forever most likely will be the person who hurts you the most."

"So what are you saying? That people shouldn't get married?"

"No, that's not what I'm saying. I'm saying it shouldn't be a day of pretend. It should be a day of truth, a day when the risks are known by all and entered in with no blinders on."

"I'm not asking you to pretend to get married. I'm asking you to pretend to be the annoying kid sister playing detective."

"And I'm telling you I don't pretend at anything."

"Not even if it will save your life?"

She backed up a step and crossed her arms. "Wade, I drive race cars. Every time I get behind the wheel, I know that I could die. I can do what I do because I keep it real."

"But, Lacey..." Wade moved in and took the sides of her face into his hands. He wanted her full attention so there wouldn't be any more dispute on the matter. "I don't know what the reality is in this situation. I can't keep it real for you, and that puts your life at more of a risk that I won't take. Don't ask me to, please."

Lacey's eyes flitted from left to right. Slowly the heat of anger lifted to indecision. Her lashes fell to her cheeks as her body struggled to hold on to its fighting stance. Her forehead fell forward to touch his, rolling back and forth.

He needed her to surrender. "Lacey, I promise to do whatever I can to honor Jeff's death. I won't forget him or your intention to find justice for him. I will make it right."

She lifted her head. Could she see the truth of his words? He meant what he said.

Birds chirped overhead as Lacey met him head-on. He admired her courage. Letting go of the course she was on would take more bravery than anything she'd already faced. It would require her to believe in him. And that was something Lacey didn't do easily...because very few had believed in her.

Wade removed his hands. The first drifted to his side, the other fell to her forearm still at her front. He wished he had the time to prove to her that the people who'd let her down had been wrong. But then, had he really treated her any differently up to this point? If anything, he'd made it known he thought her motto on life was ridiculous. Or, how had he put it?

A liability.

That *she* was a liability.

Wade backed away and started walking again. He had no right to prove anything to her.

Lacey fell in beside him with Promise, but remained quiet. After a few moments, she said, "Wade?"

"What?" He heard the hard clip in his voice. But she didn't know the annoyance was directed at himself for his wrong thinking of her.

Before he could apologize, she continued, "Jeff's voice is gone."

Wade halted at her unexpected words, but mostly from the tremor in her voice. "What do you mean?"

"I mean, Jeff was always giving me pointers and directions, and I think they're so ingrained in my head that I still hear them. Like when that guy grabbed me at the train station yesterday morning, I could hear Jeff's voice plain as day telling me what to do. But..." She looked down at her hands, and then looked back at him with more fear than he had seen in her yet. More than when she'd been shot. More than when he'd found her in the tree after being chased through the swamps.

But why the fear now?

Was it because he asked her to let go of finding justice for Jeff? For her, did that mean letting go of Jeff, as well?

The truth now stared him in the face. He reached for her hand, so cold to his touch. "I think I understand. You don't hear him anymore because you think you're giving up on him."

Quick nods of fright. "It's as if I'm driving blind. I don't know what he would want me to do in this situation. I don't hear any of his directions that got me out of so many scrapes in the past."

Wade started walking again. "We have to keep moving. You'll be safe soon, and that's what Jeff would want for you. You're making the right choice. You've got to go with that."

"Then, why get me involved in the first place? Why leave me your information so that I go looking for you? Why leave me a key to a letter in *my* name? Why prep me with self-defense skills this past year? Don't you see? Up until this point, I've been doing exactly what he would want me to do, even though he's not here to spot me anymore."

"Maybe you've done all he wanted you to do, and now it's up to me to take over."

Silence descended as they reached the back entrance of a large garage. A one-floor home was tucked out back. Lacey's childhood home, a sunny yellow, looked cozy and inviting. Numerous dormant flower beds filled the grounds, but Wade knew, come spring, they wouldn't be tended by Lacey. Flowers weren't her thing.

She reached up on her tiptoes for a lamp and withdrew a key to unlock the door. They entered a long, silent hallway.

"First door on the left is...*was* Jeff's office. Mine is across the hall on the right. But there's nothing in there that will help us."

"There's no us. You need to accept that."

"Maybe. But that doesn't change the fact that I have questions I want answered. We both are seeking the truth. We both want our reality back so we can move forward."

In the hall, nothing but the light from a red exit sign illuminated their path. It cast a reddish hue on Lacey's face and shadows below her imploring eyes. She wanted him to say she could continue this mission with him.

"I would never forgive myself if you died, Lacey. Something tells me it would be the last straw in this half existence of mine."

She turned on a sigh and led him to Jeff's office. The room practically shone. No surprise there. The guy was precise and organized in everything he did. Why wouldn't he be in his family's business?

"Everything is as he left it. No one's been ready to go through his things yet. The only reason I found the envelope with the key was because I needed the title of a car we had been working on together. He'd found a buyer for it right before he died, and I needed it to complete the transaction. I opened the file, and there was the envelope with your name in it."

Wade directed her attention to the computer on the desk. "Do you think he'd leave any other clues in there?"

"You're welcome to look, but I don't see Jeff being so careless."

"You're right. He wouldn't be." Wade scanned the small office. His eyes fell on a bookshelf that housed a selection of pictures. One grabbed his attention of Jeff and Lacey. Big brother had an arm around Lacey, pulling her in close. In addition to her headset, she wore a huge smile on her face as Jeff held up a trophy. They stood in front of a blue 1970 Firebird Trans Am.

"His pride and joy," Wade said.

Lacey lifted the picture and held it with both hands. "He loved that car."

"I wasn't talking about the car." Wade watched tears pool up in her eyes. Her pupils grew wide, and a whoosh of air escaped her lips. A myriad of questions crossed her face, but the answers couldn't be divulged in mere minutes. "He talked about you all the time."

Her brown eyes brightened. "What'd he say?"

"Lots, but the gist was that he wouldn't be the man he was without his kid sister cheering him on. Maybe someday I can write it all down for you."

She put the frame back. "I would like that."

Promise chose that moment to nudge Lacey's thigh. Wade still couldn't get over her attentiveness to Lacey. It was more than her ability to sense danger. She also sensed Lacey's pain.

Lacey bent down and burrowed her face in Promise's neck. "I'm going to miss you, you good dog." Lacey lifted her gaze to Wade, finally accepting this was the end of the road for her. "But I'm holding you to your promise to write Jeff's words down."

Wade nodded. "When this whole thing is over."

She nodded with resignation. "Before you leave, do you want to see his car?"

Wade really needed to separate from her to show the men who were following her she was inconsequential in this whole thing, but instead he said, "I wouldn't feel right leaving without at least meeting his baby."

"He really *did* tell you things." Lacey gained her feet.

"I don't say much, but when I do, you can count it as truth."

She gave him a slow smile that turned into a beacon of stunning radiance. Especially since Wade believed it to be the first smile he'd seen meant for him on her pretty lips.

A few seconds went by before he realized he was staring. A quick shake to his head cleared the haze. "We should get going."

"Oh, right. Right this way." They left the office and walked down the hall to where it opened to a four-bay garage. Over to the far right, a car was parked, shrouded, but the outline was unmistakable.

The two worked the cover off, and Wade was speechless as the metallic blue Firebird sparkled before him.

He walked around the American muscle in slow steps. "She's beautiful. He did such a nice job restoring her. And you did, too, for that matter. Jeff told me how you worked on her while he was deployed. How you helped find some of the original parts."

"Yes, there were only fifty-nine of these built with a four-speed..." Her eyes squinted. "Wait just a second... Your uncle said you didn't like cars. You don't race them, and you don't like them. Perhaps you're not being totally honest with your family."

"May I sit behind the wheel?"

"Not until you answer me. Are you hiding something from your family?"

"You don't understand. My sister hated that I left home and the business. If she knew, she would never let me leave again. It's best this—"

"Don't you dare use that line on me again. I can't believe this. You didn't even cringe about the loss of the Ferrari."

"I was crying on the inside. Trust me. Now can I sit behind the wheel? You know what? Never mind. I need to get moving anyway. Maybe some other time."

"No, here, get in," she said in a rush, opening the door. Steel bars blocked his entry. "You have to climb over them. They're a must for racing."

"I know."

"Right. Your sister would be so mad if she were here." Lacey sounded miffed as he made himself comfortable in the driver's seat.

Wade just smiled as he took in the pristine blue leather interior. Lacey reached down to the floorboard beside him, her smooth, pale neck brushed the top of his hand where he held the wheel. For a few seconds his breathing halted as his hands gripped tighter. The gorgeous car he sat in paled against the gorgeous girl beside him. The idea of reaching for her, kissing her, blindsided him.

The sound of the hood popping open jarred him back to reality. Lacey left his side and went around the front to lift the hood wide, latching it. One second she was there in front of him, the next, the hood blocked his view of her.

Wade climbed from the car, needing to be near her in these last moments together. At the same time he knew he was playing with fire. This was his friend's sister. He'd already gotten Jeff killed. Letting Lacey believe there was something between them would only hurt her, too. He was leaving. Kissing her had no point. Wade couldn't go there. It would be totally selfish of him. What was wrong with him? He had nothing to offer her.

But as he came around the front and saw her hovering over the engine, the need to take the hand she used to point something out in the engine overpowered him. The image of saying goodbye to her in his arms was one image he wanted in his mind.

The visual was absurd, but also felt like a must, a final chance at being whole. When in reality it was a dangerous course that went nowhere.

And hadn't she wanted him to keep it real?

Wade looked away from her lips. They were moving as she explained about some part she had a hard time getting. Wade nodded to show he was listening, and he was trying to. He even followed her hand when she touched the battery.

It was a strong hand, he noticed. And pretty. Quickly, he stopped that train of thought and forced his eyes to move off to her hand's right side.

Something black protruded off the battery's side. He couldn't fathom what purpose it would have on there and automatically reached down into the engine for it.

"What's this?" He cut her off as his hand pulled a piece of plastic adhered to the battery by Velcro.

Wade shot a look at Lacey's widening eyes when he realized what he held.

A USB flash drive.

She grabbed it from him and raced to the closest computer at the front desk, Wade right on her heels.

Jeff may have been smart enough not to leave info for

them on his computer, but he did leave it for them somewhere. What had Jeff found out? Was Wade's life about to finally make sense?

"It's password protected," Lacey said, tapping the keys with possible ideas. "Think. Think. What would Jeffrey use?"

"Birth date, maybe?" Wade suggested. "Not that I'm expecting that to work."

Which it didn't.

Lacey punched in another idea. "Maybe the date of the accident. What was it again? July 26, right?"

"Affirmative," Wade replied as Lacey input every possible way to write a date, even backward.

"We're going down the wrong path. He wouldn't make it this hard by making me guess. That'd be too risky. What if I never got it? He would give it to me somehow, leave it somewhere."

"In the file you found the envelope and key in? Was there anything else in there? Something that didn't look like it belonged?"

"No. Just your name and the key."

"The key, and of course the letter that the key unlocked."

Lacey jumped to her feet and reached into her jeans pocket. "The letter!" She withdrew a crumpled, soggy wad of paper. "What's left of it after the swamps anyway." She dropped to her seat and tried to unfold it.

"Easy with it," Wade instructed. "You might be able to salvage it if you're careful. We have a saying in the army. Slow is smooth and smooth is fast."

Lacey smirked. "Your idea of fast is not mine," she replied, but did slow her fingers down to attempt to keep the paper together.

Still, the message was a smeared mess.

Wade took the paper. "Don't look so upset. Something tells me you memorized most of it anyway."

She closed her eyes and started at the top from memory. "'Dear Lacey, if you're reading this then I'm d-dead.'" Her throat closed instantly. She shot a startled look up at him as if he could stop the onslaught of tears she could feel mounting rapidly. "I can't… I'm sorry. Reading it is so much different than saying it out loud."

Wade dropped to his knees. "No, I'm sorry. I wasn't thinking." He cupped the sides of her face and brought her forehead to his. She felt his thumbs rubbing the tears spilling onto her cheeks in an influx she didn't see coming and couldn't hold back. It was a culmination of the whole traumatic situation, starting with the doorbell ringing on the day she was notified of Jeffrey's death and ending in these farewell moments with Wade. In a few minutes he would walk out of her life forever. The thought brought a fresh wave of tears she wouldn't have believed existed.

Why? Why did the idea of Wade leaving her hurt so much? Was it more than the fact that he was her last link to Jeffrey? Was it because Jeff cared about his friend, and so should she? Or because she did care about him, regardless of Jeff?

"Don't worry, Lacey. I think I can remember it all. You don't have to put yourself through this."

"I'm not the one putting myself through anything. I didn't ask for any of this. But I know, someday, I'm going to have to face what I haven't wanted to if I'm ever going to make it." Lacey sniffed and stared into his intense blues. Did she dare say more? Her mother would chide her for not minding her own business, but since when did she listen to Adelaide's words of wisdom?

Lacey lifted her face to his. She pushed the tears from her cheeks and sniffed. "That goes for you, too, Wade. You can't hold your pain in forever. You'll have to talk about what you haven't wanted to face so you can move on, too."

Wade shrunk back, his face hardening against her advice.

She pointed to the letter. "If you won't listen to me, then listen to Jeff. He had a message for you, too, in there. He reminded you that words were powerful. He wanted you to find healing by talking."

"Not a chance. There are things you don't share with another human being. It would be cruel." He grabbed the paper and seemed to be using it as a means to shut her out. "Type in *wordsarepowerful*."

Lacey let him change the subject back to their task and pressed the keys.

But the code was another no-go.

They tried more of the letter's messages, including *gohome*, but nothing worked.

"All we have left are the GPS coordinates," Wade said. "But they're smeared."

"Were they saved in your watch from when you typed them in?"

Wade searched to find out, and after a minute brought them up so she could quickly type them in.

"Bingo! We're in," she announced on a gasp of excitement. "Thank you, Jeff. This letter wasn't useless after all."

Wade took the seat beside her while she pulled the files on the USB drive up on the screen. The first file was some sort of legal document. She quickly realized what she was looking at after watching her friends receive forms just like this one. She shot a glance at Wade, dread filtering in as he read it, too.

With full attention, his eyes roved over the first paragraph. The horror on his face said he'd already comprehended, but he had yet to speak.

She stated the obvious. "They're divorce papers."

Wade's lips curled. "My mom filed for divorce?"

Lacey pointed at the screen. "Your dad. A month before the accident, it looks like."

"So he knew his wife was doing something illegal."

"It doesn't say why."

"It doesn't have to." Wade's angry edge spiked back into his voice.

As he came to grips with this puzzle piece, Lacey opened the next file. A slew of newspaper clippings scrolled down the screen. One after another spoke about the town of Norcastle and the economic decline of the area and loss of jobs. Lacey arrowed down through them until she came to an article with a photo. The headline read, Racetrack to Save Town!

"Is that your mom?" Lacey asked.

Wade squinted at the screen with a stiff nod. "It's grainy, but it looks like the ribbon-cutting ceremony of Spencer Speedway. That's my dad on one side of her, and Clay on the other."

"He still looks the same. Just as kind looking as when I met him."

"He's a good guy." Wade shook his head with a disgusted look. "I wish Roni would see that and stop fighting him on every little detail. He stepped in for our parents, and he's stepped in for me more times than I can count. Always said my job at the track would be there when I'm ready. *If* I'm ready. And he's okay if it never happens. He's done a better job running the place than I ever would have." Wade grew quiet. "I wonder if he knew about the divorce."

"Maybe. Looks as if your parents involved him in the start-up of the business. They had to be close. But who's the other guy in the picture?"

Wade leaned in. "What other guy?"

"The one standing on the platform in the background. He's wearing some sort of pin." Lacey squinted. "Vote for Jobs, it says. A political campaign?"

"Can't tell. Some politician, I suppose. Norcastle went through some troubling times economically. The racetrack was the beginning of the town's restoration. People were excited to have it come and bring jobs, but it did need to be approved at the town and state levels."

Lacey closed the file and opened the next. A picture of a racetrack came up first. "The date stamped on these is from August of this year. Jeff must have taken them."

Wade leaned in. "They're of my family's track. Jeff was at the speedway? He never told me he went there."

"Well, you asked him for his help. He was being thorough, I'm sure. Nothing wrong with that." Lacey couldn't hold back the edge in her voice. She didn't like the implication that Jeff had been secretive with Wade. She scrolled down the pictures, not really seeing anything out of the ordinary. A bunch of cars. A grandstand. An office hut. An old dairy truck. A bunch of letters written on the side of the truck.

"He was supposed to send me everything he found. That's why we set up the dead drop. That was the system. He's had these files for months. Why didn't he send them to me?"

"Maybe because they're a bunch of pictures from your track. Pictures you can go out and take anytime. *If* you ever went home."

Wade shot her a warning glare. She'd gone too far… again. *Sorry, Mama.*

Lacey reined it in. "All I'm saying is why would Jeff bother sending you photos of your own property? Kind of a waste of a trip to your locker in Virginia if you could go take the pics yourself, don't you think?" Lacey calmed her voice but still didn't like Wade insinuating that Jeffrey had betrayed him. Her brother wasn't here to defend himself. She would do it for him.

"What about the divorce papers? Why hadn't he shared those?"

"Simple. He didn't see a point yet in sharing the divorce with you. He wouldn't have caused you unnecessary hurt."

"It was the system we set up to follow. It was the plan."

Lacey looked to the ceiling in exasperation. "You and your plans. That's not how life works, Wade."

"Neither does winging it." Wade grabbed the mouse from her hand and clicked to open the last file. In the next second, Wade shot back. His face paled before her, and his dimple disappeared in a shocked, speechless face.

Lacey faced the screen and read the heading of some sort of document aloud. "'*A Russian Spy at an American Racetrack*, by US Army Warrant Officer Jeffrey Phillips.'"

Lacey felt as though she'd just rammed her car into a wall. Her sweet, kind brother, whom she had just been defending, had been writing a book at Wade's expense?

A click from behind broke their stunned silence, followed by a lethal growl from Promise that Lacey wouldn't have ever thought she had in her. In the next second, Promise jumped on Lacey and pushed her down to the floor. Like a team, Wade maneuvered in front of Lacey to block her from the intruder who had just cocked a gun.

NINE

"Put your hands up where I can see them," the gun holder said.

Wade went for his own gun, forgetting again that he didn't have it on him anymore. More than a little miffed, he followed orders and raised his hands.

"Daddy! Don't shoot! It's me," Lacey shouted from the floor behind Wade. Promise had her pinned down, covering her with her seventy-pound body.

Lacey's words hit him before he could fathom again Promise's response to protect her.

This guy was Lacey's father?

Wade dropped his arms and offered one for a handshake. "Mr. Phillips, I'm Wade Spencer."

"I don't care who you are. Get away from my daughter. Did you take her?"

"Take her?"

"No, Daddy, he didn't." Lacey spit dog hair out of her mouth. "Wade, can you get your dog off me so I can clear this up?"

Wade gave a whistle and Promise hopped off Lacey, but the dog stayed tense and at the ready. She gave another growl, baring her teeth.

Lacey pushed to her feet. "I'm fine, Dad. I would have called, but these guys—"

"But we lost our phones," Wade cut in before she went too far. The less information they offered, the safer everyone would be.

"No, Wade—" Lacey touched his arm "—my dad can be trusted. Wade, meet my dad, Frank. Daddy, Wade."

Frank Phillips kept his gun on him. Not that Wade faulted the man. The guy's daughter had been missing since Christmas Eve. Take that into account with the fact that he'd just lost his son, and security would be beefed up around here with all barrels pointed at the new guy.

"Wade's not one of the bad guys, Daddy. He was Jeffrey's friend. He's helping me figure out what happened to Jeff." Lacey stepped up to her father. Within five seconds the gun was lowered and the man had his other arm securely wrapped around his daughter. He pressed his cheek into her mangled hair.

"I didn't know what to think when you didn't come home for Christmas. I had a bear of a time placating your mother."

"I can only imagine," Lacey said with her voice muffled in his gray mechanic shirt. "She only takes out the fine china on every day that ends in *y*."

"I'm being serious. She wanted me to call the police, and if I didn't hear from you by noon today, I was going to." The man glanced over her head at Wade. Doubt still filled his eyes. "Who are these guys? And I want the truth."

"Sir, I'll give you the truth, but for your safety it's best if you don't know all of it."

A resigned sigh escaped him. "That bad?"

Wade looked at Lacey, and her father got the gist of the danger. He tightened his hold for a few minutes as he decided what he would do next.

"Your mother has been a wreck since I told her why

you left. She just knew this new adventure of yours had *bad news* written all over it."

Lacey pulled away from her father. "Dad, we talked about this when I showed you the envelope. You know I had no choice but to go. It's what Jeff wanted me to do." She looked over at the computer screen with the manuscript still open. "Even though I'm not sure if I trust any of Jeff's directions for me right now. I'm a little disappointed in him at the moment."

Mr. Phillips's eyebrow's lifted at his daughter. "Why would you say such a thing about your brother?"

She dropped her attention to fiddle with a button on Cora's shirt. Wade knew exactly why she hesitated. "Jeff was a trait—"

"Trainer," Wade cut her off again. "He was always pretty tough on her, pushing her, training her to beat anyone she came up against. He told me all about it. He wanted her to be the best. Not just the best girl, but the best, overall. Lacey doesn't think she'll ever measure up. That she'll always have something to prove."

Mr. Phillips frowned down at Lacey. "I warned Jeff. I told him he expected too much from you. That he would make you feel inadequate if you couldn't reach that place of honor he set so high for you. But, honey, don't hold it against him. He loved you. More than anything in this world."

Lacey looked over at Wade, gratitude filled her tear-sheened eyes. "I know he did."

Wade offered her a quick nod. He might feel Jeff's knife twisting in his back, but he wasn't about to ruin a father's memory of his dead son. No matter if that son had tried to exploit Wade's family.

"Lacey!" A screech echoed to the rafters of the shop. Before Wade could turn around to see who made that high-pitched noise, he watched Lacey's shining eyes scrunch closed.

Then she opened them and swung around to greet the petite woman who resembled Lacey to a T, except for the perfectly styled rich brown hair, bright pink feminine dress and three-inch heels that stomped across the smooth concrete with a vengeance.

"Hey, Mama," Lacey said. "I'm home."

Adelaide Phillips reached her arms out for Lacey for a quick, hard hug, then brought them back to cross them at her front in a "mama ain't happy" fashion. "When your father told me that you weren't coming to Christmas because you took off to New Hampshire, and that you hadn't checked in, I just knew this was another one of your dangerous escapades. You're making me gray with all this worrying for your safety."

"There's no need to worry," Lacey said. The words were useless. Lacey knew her mother would always worry about anything she did. "I've had Wade here keeping an eye on everything." Adelaide took notice of Wade for the first time since she entered. "I just couldn't call because we're without a phone right now." Lacey continued speaking, but her mother's attention was diverted for the moment.

"Is he your boyfriend?" Adelaide asked, still looking at Wade.

Lacey sputtered, "No way. You know that's not my style."

Adelaide shot her attention back to Lacey. She dropped her gaze to Cora's blouse. "Neither are flowers."

"It's not my shirt. I had to borrow it when I was shot." Lacey cringed, knowing she went too far…again.

Adelaide's mouth dropped. "You were *what*? Did you

say you were shot? As in with a *gun*?" Tears filled her mother's eyes; her hand covered her mouth. "Oh, Frank, did you hear her? She could have been killed."

Frank stepped up behind his wife. Lacey expected her dad to be on her side like he always was when she sparred with her mother. But this time the anger on his face said otherwise. "You didn't tell me you'd taken a bullet."

"First, I didn't get a chance to before Mama came in. Second, I didn't *take* a bullet. It grazed my arm. I'm fine. And third, these are the same musclemen who killed Jeff. I'm going to get them, Daddy. I won't stop until I do."

"Death will stop you," Adelaide said, debate over. Once again, Adelaide won with her wisdom. "Did you even think that if you died, we would have to bury our second child within a month of our first?" Adelaide swallowed, tears rimmed her eyes and her dainty hand covered her quivering mouth. Lacey thought her mother even cried pretty. Adelaide swiped a trail from her cheek so delicately.

They were so different, the two of them. Night and day. Lacey remembered when her brother died and what her reflection in the mirror looked like, all puffy and red. She was nothing like her mother in the looks department. And apparently in the brains, either.

Lacey dropped her gaze to the floor. "No, I wasn't thinking about that possibility. I guess I failed you again."

Adelaide sobered. "Failed me? What is that supposed to mean? You haven't failed me."

"I'm your disappointment. I'll never be like you. I'll never be the debutante daughter you always wanted who sits on the porch swing for afternoon sweet tea. I'll always sport perpetual helmet hair and choose a fire-retardant suit over dresses."

Adelaide gave a small laugh and reached to lift Lacey's

chin. "Honey, I accepted a long time ago that gowns and updos were out of the picture. I saw our blaring differences early on, but that doesn't mean I thought less of you or was disappointed in you. You were still my little girl, and I just wanted you to be safe, to make good choices in your life."

"As in stop racing. That's what you mean, isn't it? I know you hate it every time I get behind the wheel. That's never going to change, Mama. This is who I am."

"Do my dresses make you love me less?"

"Of course not."

"Well, your fire-retardant suit doesn't make me love you less, either. Nothing you could ever do, or not do, or wear, or say, will change the way I feel about you. I will always love you." Adelaide laid her hand on Lacey's chest. "I love you for the woman you are in here."

"Then, trust me that I can do this. I'm going to prove Jeff was murdered and bring his killers to justice. We just found a clue and were about to go follow it."

Wade cleared his throat beside her. "No, you're not. Your mom might not stop you, but I will. You're not coming with me. It's not safe."

Adelaide turned her attention to Wade. "Wade, is it? Son, I've made that argument till I was blue in the face. You see where it got me, right? Sometimes you have to trust God and let go." Adelaide turned to the key holder and grabbed a key with a bluebird key ring. "Now, you're going to need a car."

Lacey inhaled. "No, Mama! I can't take Jeff's car."

"Oh, yes, you can. Muscle thugs call for the snarl of a souped-up muscle car. Besides, that baby is like a tank. If you're going to drive out of here into danger, then I want you to have the safest car in the shop." She held the keys out to Wade, but Lacey threw an arm out to grab them before he could.

"I'll take those. He can ride shotgun. The man owns a racetrack, but his pedal never hits the floor. Daddy, we need a gun. Can we take yours?"

Frank passed his gun over to her. She checked the barrel and passed it over to Wade.

"I really don't like this idea," Wade said. "Lacey, you should stay here. Call the police and let them protect you."

Adelaide smiled at Wade. "I like you, Wade. Lacey, listen to him. He knows what he's talking about."

"I think it's too late for that," Frank said from the front of the garage. She hadn't even noticed her dad walk to the front to peer out the small square bay windows. "We've got company. A black SUV is cruising by as slow as snail snot. Friends of yours?"

Lacey looked back at Wade. "You were saying? It's not safe for me here, either. They found us. Grab the USB and get in the car."

"They're trolling. They've got to be." Wade pocketed the drive and raced to the window to peer out from the edge. "They can't know we're here. How could they?"

"Doesn't matter. Let's go." Lacey grabbed Wade's coat off the chair and reached the car. She jumped into the driver's seat.

"Wait! If we come tearing out of here, they'll be on us from the word *go*. There's no way we'll lose them. We need to think about this."

"No time for a conference call, Wade! And we can't stay in here waiting for them to break down the door, either. Get in the car!"

Wade made his way to the Trans Am's passenger side.

Promise jumped in over the steel cage and parked it on the floor of the passenger seat.

"Daddy!" Lacey called from her open door. "As soon as I start the engine, open the bay. Mama, call the police."

Adelaide held the phone up to show she was already one step ahead…as usual.

Lacey slammed the door. "Wade, crack the window and get that gun ready. You have some tires to shoot out, but try to wait until we get to the bridge. Let's get them as far away from my parents as possible."

He nodded and brought the window down enough to fit the barrel out. "Ready."

Lacey turned the engine over. The Firebird Trans Am roared to life like an angry lion being woken up in the middle of his sleep. The deep rumble echoed off the concrete garage walls.

Wade shook his head. "Great. They'll hear us coming from miles away."

"Yes, but there's no way they'll catch us, so who cares?"

And with that, she floored it out of the bay just as the door lifted enough to clear it. At the end of the parking lot, Lacey took a right, her tires squealing on the pavement. The view in her rearview mirror was clear. She looked again to be sure.

Empty.

"Where'd they go?" she yelled. "Did we get away before they saw us?"

As if on cue, the SUV shot out from a side street directly behind her. She'd spoken too soon, and this time she wouldn't be getting a three-tap warning.

TEN

"Where are you going?" Wade shouted when Lacey took an unexpected sharp turn onto a narrow road off the main drag.

"A shortcut to the bridge. We need to get to the expressway and over the Wando River to Charleston." She glanced in her rearview mirror. "They didn't turn. Maybe we shook them."

Wade kept his eyes on the passenger-side mirror and muttered, "I wish I was driving."

Lacey made a noise like a tire releasing air. "With the way you drive, we wouldn't have made it out of the parking lot of the shop before being ambushed."

"Some would call my driving detailed."

"I would call it slow. Any sign of them?" She took another sharp, screeching turn that had Wade bracing himself in his seat.

"Negative, but could you warn me next— Lacey! On your right!"

The black SUV rocketed out of a side street directly in front of them, cutting them off. The Trans Am's brakes locked up to a fishtailing stop. Lacey switched gears and had the car careening down another street. A look in the mirror showed the bouncing headlights of the SUV coming up right behind them.

"They're on us," he warned.

"How do they know these back roads? I thought for sure I'd lose them." Lacey banged the steering wheel with the palm of her left hand. "It was as if they knew exactly where I was headed. I don't get it."

"Don't try to. Just drive. Get us to the bridge."

Lacey shifted the stick and the car roared to the next gear, sending them flying down the street. She picked up another side street.

Wade spotted the SUV one block over, heading in the same direction, driving parallel to them. The bridge came into view ahead. "They're trying to beat us to the bridge to cut us off. Go!"

"I love that word," she said.

Wade turned his head away from the window to judge her profile. "I think you're enjoying this too much. This isn't your typical race, you know. If you lose this one, we die."

"Lose?" She shifted again. "I'm sorry, I don't understand."

They exited the street and raced to the expressway.

"Get your gun ready," Lacey said, calm and collected, as she looked into her rearview mirror. "They're coming up on my left. As soon as they reach us, I'll switch lanes so they're on your side."

With the SUV in place, Lacey hit the brakes and the SUV continued to drive forward past them. She quickly cranked the wheel left to fall in behind the SUV, making her now the chaser.

Wade whistled. "That was smooth."

"What were you saying about slow being smooth?"

"Nothing. Never mind."

The SUV led the way onto the bridge and out over the river.

"He's biding his time. Any second now, he's going to brake to make us either hit him or attempt not to, which could land us in the river if we go over the concrete barrier. I, for one, am not up for a swim."

"So then back off."

"Back off? You keep speaking another language to me."

Lacey wrenched the wheel to the left and came up on the left side of the SUV. There was barely any room to fit, but no big deal. She squeezed in, door handle to door handle. "Can you see any faces?"

"The windows are tinted. All I can see is an outline of their heads."

Just then the SUV driver whipped the wheel to smash into the side of the Trans Am.

"Oh, you want to swap paint, do you?" Lacey yelled and rammed back. "How does that feel? We have a steel cage taking the shock. What do you have?"

The window cracked, and the barrel of a gun appeared.

"Time to go," she said, and hit the gas to pull out in front of them at high speed. "Now, Wade! Kill their tires!"

Wade was already taking aim at the wheels. Two shots blew out both the driver's-side tires, sending the SUV in a spin, then a flip. It skidded on its rooftop toward the concrete barrier. Sparks flew and so did seconds as they waited to see the outcome in their mirrors.

The truck slammed into the wall and lifted onto its front end. Wade's lungs burned as he held his breath. The SUV seemed to hover straight up in the air as its momentum decided if it was strong enough to continue over the barrier.

Then the vehicle slammed back down on the road.

Lacey banged her fist on the wheel again. "So close!"

"Not to worry. They won't be going anywhere for a while. Let's get out of here before any witnesses turn us in. At least morning rush hour is over and the bridge is nearly empty."

"Do you think we're free, then? We can stop looking over our shoulder?"

"Just drive. I'll do the watching, but yes, I think we have a small breather. And if we change up our direction every few hours, it should stay that way. They won't know where we're heading or where to cut us off like last time."

"I doubt they'll even find us."

"They found us at your family's shop. They knew to go there and not the house."

"Yeah, that is weird."

"Weird, or they've found a way to track us." Wade touched the buckle of his GPS watch. Had they figured out he had one and found a way to use it to their advantage? Whether or not they had, he rolled down his window and made the decision to let it go.

"Bridge," Wade reminded her again from the passenger side of the darkened car.

"Oops, sorry, I'm getting tired." Lacey hit the blinker and changed lanes just as they passed under the overpass. "You would think I would be used to changing lanes under the bridges after thirty hours of driving with you. Are you ever going to tell me why I have to switch lanes under every overpass? Don't get me wrong, it's great practice for racing, especially during heavy traffic, but I would still love to know why you want me to do it."

"I told you the last time you asked. You won't understand."

Lacey gave up and kept driving into the night. She looked to where Wade held the gun on his right thigh.

He'd kept it at the ready since she handed it off to him. Now, after all these quick lane changes for no apparent reason, she had to wonder if giving him the gun had been a good idea.

She decided to ask another question he probably wouldn't answer, either. "Why doesn't your sister want you to carry a weapon?"

"And here I thought Questions was gone for good."

"Not until Secrets is."

"I don't keep silent about things because I want to keep secrets. It's for your own protection."

"I'm tough, Wade. I can handle it. I've seen death, you know. Drivers don't always come away from a race."

After a few minutes of more silence, other than Promise's snoring from the passenger-side floor, he said, "Overseas the insurgents throw bombs off the bridges just as you're driving under them. I've seen enough of my men in their Humvees explode under a bridge to be wary. You get used to switching lanes to stay alive. The habit stays with you even after you return home."

Lacey felt her eyes widen. She hadn't been expecting that as an answer to her question. "I see." Her voice sounded low and deep in the quiet cabin. She looked off to the next overpass coming closer and got ready to change lanes again. "I don't think I'll ever look at another bridge the same way." Wade faced forward, nothing but the dashboard lights illuminating his face. "Thank you for sharing, Wade. And thank you for your sacrifice."

"You're welcome, but it wasn't a sacrifice. I consider it an honor to serve my country with so many courageous people. Many I will miss greatly."

Wade wrapped his hand around the butt of the gun. It fit like a glove.

"But they didn't all die during their tours, did they?"

He shot her a look, eyes blinking, before he shook his head. "Some can't come back and start over again."

"And that's why the army gave you Promise, and why your sister doesn't want you carrying."

He gave a short nod before looking out the passenger window.

Promise whined and stirred from her slumber at Wade's feet. He reached down with his free hand and patted her. "I'm okay, girl."

"She senses you even in her sleep."

"She's woken me up from many a nightmare. Flips on the lights and everything."

Lacey wondered what those dreams entailed. How far to the edge they might push him. "Does your sister's worry about you carrying a gun have weight?"

"No," he answered quickly. "But she doesn't believe me. I would never take my life. I've seen too much death. I cherish life too much to even think it. I have hope that tomorrow will be better."

Lacey looked back to the open road in front of her. "I believe you." And she did. The way he took protecting her so seriously, when he didn't even know her, told her so. "What kind of things do you do in the army?"

"Typical stuff."

"Like?"

He shrugged. "Rescues, rappelling, reports. Lots of reports."

"Rappelling? Like off cliffs?"

"No. Out of helicopters."

"Really? No way!"

Wade laughed, the sound so rich and pleasant it lifted the mood around them. She realized it was the first real laugh she'd heard from him since they met. She could listen to it for hours, but the chances of hearing it again were probably nil.

"So how does one rappel?" she asked. "Throw a rope out and slide down?"

"It's a little more detailed than that. Or you die. I told you I cherish life, didn't I?"

"More detailed? Just up your alley, then. You do like your plans and stuff."

He smiled big her way, and his dimple popped, but no laugh.

Too bad.

"Take the next right," he said. "We're back."

The sign for entering Norcastle shone in the headlights. It seemed so long ago when they'd raced out of there, but that could be because she felt as though they'd traveled the whole country since they'd left. With all their false turns and alternative routes to trick their pursuers, it took them a lot longer to get here than Lacey's first trip up north. But the detours were necessary to stay alive.

"It's so peaceful up in these mountains," Lacey said as she leaned forward over the steering wheel to look up and out the window. "Those stars are amazing. I missed them the first time coming here."

"You have an excuse. You were being followed."

"True, but even though I had unwanted company, I still liked the feeling of your town," she told him. "There's just something strong and resilient about it. Really community oriented. It probably helped me stay calm and focused, and I didn't even realize it. I feel as if I've stepped back in time to the late 1800s. Especially with the Victorian architecture of your town hall and the opera house at the village's center. I really like how everyone decked their homes in Christmas lights, too. It's festive and welcoming."

"The buildings have had a lot of work done to them in the past twenty years," he said. "Before that, the place was nearly in ruins. Picture the factories along the river with busted windows and a lot of spray paint. You wouldn't have felt very welcome if you came then. The place was desolate. After the factories closed, people left everything behind and moved away."

"Then your parents arrived and opened a racetrack. Those newspaper clippings my brother put on the flash drive say Spencer Speedway was here to save the town. It looks as if it did."

Lacey looked out at the many lights filling the windows of the factories, now turned into lofts, apartments, inns and restaurants. She sensed no failure to thrive roaming through these downtown streets. Only new life.

"It's more than what you see, too," Wade said. "It's more than jobs for the community. Whole families have been brought together through racing. It's a common bond that tightens their relationships, except if you're the owners' kids. Our family was obliterated." Bitterness showed through Wade's smirk. "When I see the fruit of what my parents started, particularly my mom, who had the vision for all this in the first place, I get stumped. How could someone do so much good and bad at the same time?"

Lacey took in the town. Meredith had a love for racing but also family and community. Why? "You're right, Wade. It doesn't jibe. I'm thinking you might be wrong about your mom."

"You saw your brother's manuscript. He found enough on her to write a book. *A Russian Spy at an*

American Racetrack. You saw it yourself. All of this was a cover."

"You can't know that without reading what Jeff wrote."

"I plan to as soon we get back."

"Back? Don't you mean home?"

"No. This place is not my home and never will be."

Wade was glad when Lacey left his comment alone. He shouldn't have said it in the first place. It was a slip, but explained how going home always felt like going back to the place of injury, which was why he rarely returned and only for short visits to appease his sister. Going home always meant ripping the scars off his wounds only to relive the pain all over again.

Wade closed his eyes and dropped his head back on the leather headrest. He breathed deep and felt a slobbery lick on his hand. He opened his eyes to find Promise resting her head on his seat. She'd roused from her slumber from under his feet to offer him comfort. The dog knew her duty. She was well trained at what she did. He recognized it for what it was. Lacey may say it was love, but he would recognize duty anywhere.

Mostly because of the duty he shirked on a daily basis—leaving the racetrack to his sister to run.

"Take the next right," he instructed.

"Is it a shortcut to the house?" Lacey craned her neck to scan the rearview mirror. "Are we being followed again? Did they catch up to us? How?" Panic raised her deep voice.

"No one's following us. Calm down. Your expertise took care of our company way back in South Carolina."

She smiled big and beautiful, and he let the sight clear away his doldrums.

"Why, thank you, Wade. And yours, too, by the way.

You're a great shot. Are you sure you don't want to add sniper to your duties in the army? It couldn't have been all rappelling and reports." She took the turn, looking at him eagerly for an answer. Her eyebrows arched to open vibrant, curious eyes.

Wade couldn't hold back his own smile. "I could tell you, but then I'd have to kill you." She laughed, but he let his smile go while his hand roamed over Promise's silky fur. "War is hard, Lacey. I don't even want you imagining it."

She drove in silence a mile down the road before she asked, "Where are we going?"

"To the track."

She whipped a look at him. "But isn't it closed for the season?"

"I know the owners."

"But why are we going there?"

I'm not ready to go back. "I want to check something out."

"But it's dark."

"I'll put the lights on for you, scaredy-cat."

"Who said I was scared?" She floored it, and Wade smiled in satisfaction. He would say she was predictable, but really the only thing he could count on where Lacey was concerned was her impulsivity. Hang a carrot in front of her, and she would go for it. Even hint that she had inadequacies, and she would set out to prove you wrong.

It went beyond her mother and the guys at the track. It was a constant battle she felt she needed to fight.

But then, who was he to talk? His battles raged constantly in him, too.

"What are we looking for?" Lacey asked at the parking lot of Spencer Speedway.

"It's something about those pictures your brother took

when he was here in August. I noticed he only took one picture of the track. Most of his photos were of the grandstand and the beverage truck."

"Did you tell him about how you spoke to that man under the grandstand?"

"Jeff knew all about that incident. I told him everything so he could help."

"I'm sure that's why he took pictures of the grandstand then. Over it and under it."

"But what about the beverage delivery truck? Why take so many shots of that? It's a 1961 Ford truck that's been there since it died there, long before the track opened. My parents thought it was neat and kept it as a novelty."

"I guess I need to see the pictures again. I wasn't paying too much attention to the details of the photos. Just the divorce— Sorry. Never mind."

"Don't be sorry. Jeff found out something I didn't know. Unfortunately, the divorce makes this whole scenario even more painful."

There are some hurts that last a lifetime.

Lacey cut the engine as Wade remembered his words to her on divorce. It would be good to remind himself of them, especially when he got a penchant for bringing their relationship to another level. The idea of causing that kind of pain in her life made his head spin. He would definitely be the one to hurt her.

They sat in stillness with the back side of the grandstand rising up in front of them, a black structure of immense proportions jutting up into the sky. It blocked the view to the track like the undiscovered facts of his past.

The truth of what really happened the night they had gone over the ledge. A freak accident? An assassination of a Russian spy? Or now, in light of the divorce, an aggrieved spouse looking for restitution for their pain?

Wade's throat clenched, nearly causing him to gag aloud. The idea of one of his parents purposely causing that fiery descent off the edge of the world undid him. The crash had taken forever to come. He remembered careening down the slope into the ravine, the car bouncing up and down.

It had flipped twice.

Wade had sat behind his dad, who'd driven the car. He remembered calling for him to make it stop. But when the car finally had, his dad was slumped over the wheel, his mother's head tilted unnaturally to her left, broken. Before he could reach for her, the fire had burst from the engine into the car. In one whoosh, his parents had been ensconced. Instead of reaching for his mom, he'd grabbed Roni out from the line of shooting flames.

But he hadn't been fast enough.

The fire was so hot and fast.

So hot.

So…

Water doused his hands where he touched the flames on his sister, trying to put them out.

Only there hadn't been water that day. That day he had rolled with her on the ground, trying to do what Fireman Dan had said to do when he came to visit Wade's third-grade class during Fire Prevention Week.

So where was the water coming from?

A dog barked.

A woman yelled.

"Mom!" Wade screamed with his three-year-old sister in his arms.

"Wade! It's me, Lacey!" the woman yelled again.

Lacey? Not Meredith? Not his mother.

No, of course not—his parents had been dead before the fire had even started.

Wetness covered his face, tearing Wade from his recurring memory. He opened his eyes to find Promise frantically licking him from his hands and arms to his cheeks and chin.

And behind Promise was a beautiful young woman with tears streaking down her face. She cried for him as she reached for the back of his neck. She came closer with shushing on her lips.

Lips that blinded all reason.

Wade didn't change course but zeroed in on the only thing he thought would make this all go away. He reached for the back of her messy ponytail and searched for the relief her kiss could offer him.

His kiss turned demanding when that solace never came.

And it never would come because he wasn't whole. Using Lacey felt like the dirtiest thing he'd ever done. Dirtier than any covert task he'd taken on in the military.

She was tired of proving her worth, and now he had to tell her she wouldn't heal him, either. But that wasn't her fault. She had to know this.

Wade pulled back and reached for the door handle. "I'm broken, Lacey. Dead, in fact. Deader than that beverage truck on the other side of that fence." He climbed out. "Just stay away. It's best."

Wade walked to the gate. The frigid temperature of the north restricted his chest from dragging in full breaths of painful air. He wished for the cold pain to cover his forever pain.

At the gate, he halted at what awaited him.

He thought he would have to break the lock but found it unlatched. Had it been broken into today? It could have been weeks ago. With the racing season over, Roni or Clay had no reason to be here every day.

It didn't matter. What mattered was that someone else had been here.

Someone who could still be inside.

ELEVEN

Lacey's hand trembled over her mouth where Wade had just kissed her. Somewhere beyond the myriad of questions spinning out of control in her mind like a rotating kaleidoscope, she could make out Promise whining. Lacey could hear the animal, and with a slow turn of her head, she could see the frenzied dog at the passenger door. Claws scratched on vinyl and carpet with growing urgency, pulling Lacey out of her stupor little by little until reality slammed into her as forcefully as Wade had slammed the passenger door when he left.

Right after he'd kissed her.

It had happened so fast, so unexpectedly. All she'd wanted to do was comfort him in what could only have been some sort of flashback. Some sort of memory that was so real to him and still held him so powerfully in its grip.

But he'd kissed her.

Had he thought she was eliciting that kind of response? Did he think she was leaning in to kiss him in what could have only been the most inappropriate moment she could have chosen? *If* she had chosen it, which she hadn't. She had only meant to reach out to touch him and pull his focus onto her. She'd meant to remind him he was in

present day and he was safe with her. She would never take advantage of him in such a dire-straits situation. The man was in obvious pain. He needed comfort. He needed healing. He needed…

He kissed her.

He kissed *her.*

Lacey let her hand fall from her lips. She could feel her lips swelling up from his hard touch. A touch that was desperate and fraught with need.

But what did he need?

Promise barked and whined and jumped back and forth from the floor to the seat. Her paws continued to scratch vigorously at the door.

He needed Promise. But not for her duties to him, as he always said.

"You want to go love him, don't you, Promise? I see that, but I'm sorry to say he doesn't. He's so hung up on duty that he can't recognize your unconditional love for him."

Lacey leaned over and pulled the latch. "Don't give up on him, girl. Show him he's not so broken that he can't be loved. Go." She pushed the door wide, and Promise bolted from the car. Snow swished into the air from the dog's golden-red hind legs as she raced to the gate and her handler.

But Promise didn't know Wade as her handler. She knew him as her best friend. She didn't love him out of duty or training or for anything he could do for her, but because loving him brought her joy.

"That is a Jesus kind of love," Lacey said aloud, remembering her youth pastor's words to her back in high school. Lacey had always felt the need to prove she measured up in people's eyes. Her youth pastor recognized this in her and pulled her aside one Christmas Eve. He

asked her if she understood what real love looked like. What a Jesus kind of love looked like. How God's gift of love on Christmas morning came with no strings attached, with nothing for her to prove or earn. In His eyes, she was loved beyond measure, and never had to measure up.

The idea had been so foreign to her, and yet, the comfort it gave her had her believing it wholeheartedly. She put her trust in God that night, and never became afraid to step out again, because she knew He was beside her, behind her and always guiding her. A Jesus kind of love, and it was for all.

All who accepted it, that was.

Would Wade accept God's gift of love if he couldn't even accept Promise's? It could be a turning point for him if he did. It would make all the difference in his life, as it had in hers.

But *he* kissed *her.*

What if he was looking for love from *her*? Lacey shook away the idea as absurd. He didn't even like her. He'd said so himself. She was too impulsive, a liability, even. Besides, she would never open her heart and life up to someone who rejected love from anyone, most especially his own dog. And let's not forget Wade was responsible for her brother's death, however indirectly and regardless that Jeff might have betrayed Wade by secretly writing a book. Perhaps Wade had figured that out and really did have a hand in Jeff's death as payback.

Lacey didn't believe that idea, but still, if Wade was looking for love from her, he could forget it. That was one road she said she would never go down.

But God's love was different. His love came freely to all who accepted it. Lacey couldn't withhold that from Wade as she could withhold her love. *If* she even felt

love for him, which she didn't. "I don't," she said with a slap on the steering wheel. Whatever stirred in her head when his lips were on hers wasn't love. It couldn't be. She wouldn't allow it. She'd made up her mind a long time ago to go solo. Except for God, of course. But that was different. His love would never hurt her.

Lacey sighed and dropped her head back on the headrest. "I'm assuming You want me to tell him that, God? Is that why You led me to his front door? To be Your messenger?"

Lacey took the quiet stillness as her answer and pulled the door latch to go. Deep fresh-fallen snow slowed her steps as she trudged forward in the direction Wade and Promise had gone. As she came around the corner of the ticket booth, she saw the gate had been pushed wide, but Wade and Promise were gone.

Lacey stepped into the speedway. A concession stand stood dark and off to her right. The vintage 1961 Ford beverage truck, topped with a foot of snow and words scrawled on the side that read Soda Pop Delivery in faded red letters, was parked in front of the grandstand. She remembered the photos Jeff had taken. Many were of the red letters on the truck.

But it was the towering black grandstand behind the truck that vied for her attention.

This was the grandstand that had started all of Wade's pain. It was where he'd found that capsule when he was eight years old. Where he'd told the stranger his mother had it. And just a few hours later his parents and brother had been dead.

Had Wade gone there now while his memory was so real from the flashback?

If so, this would be the perfect time to tell him he was loved beyond measure. Lacey took the first steps toward

the stands. She had a message that would change everything for him. But first she had to find him, and with no lights on in this place, she was going blind.

Wade stepped out of the office, pieces of shattered glass from the window crunching beneath the treads of his boots. The place had been ransacked, but from what he could tell, it wasn't a fresh smash and grab.

He didn't know when the last employee had been here. He also didn't know what was missing. His absence from the speedway had never felt so disconcerting. As co-owner, these were things he should know. Come daylight, Roni and Clay would have to determine if the loss exceeded the computers ripped from the desks. His sister and uncle knew more about the present running of the business than he did.

The irony struck him to his core. His whole life was about duty, yet the one duty Roni needed him most for, he shirked.

Wade closed the door but didn't bother locking it. There was no point with the window gone.

The word *messy* came to mind. Either some amateur was looking for items to hawk, or the whole scene had been set up to look like it. If that was the case, what had someone been looking for? Was it the same people after him and Lacey?

Thinking of Lacey had him picking up his steps to get back to her. He hadn't meant to leave her this long. In fact, he had promised to not leave her again after the train. He could say the busted-up office building had thrown him for a few minutes, but that wouldn't be the truth. His flashback to the accident had messed with his mind again.

And she'd witnessed it firsthand.

He had a lot to explain and apologize for, including the kiss. He quickly pressed his lips tight. The feel of her lips on his still lingered, but it couldn't happen again.

Wade headed toward the exit, but a flash of lights from the thick trees on the other side of the track stopped him. He saw two lights that quickly died out. Two lights that could only be headlights.

They'd been found.

Wade didn't know how, and at the moment, didn't care. Lacey consumed every bit of his concern. Even the sound of a dog barking faded into the background of Wade's pounding feet in the hard-packed snow, but soon, sharp, high-pitched howls had him skidding to a stop.

Was that Promise barking? She never barked unless… unless she had to alert him to danger.

Wade searched the dark paddock where, come spring, cars and their trailers would be lined up as far as the eye could see. Finding a dog should be easy. But the space lay open and covered with untouched snow. No canine tracks could be seen. No tracks at all.

Wade spun around at another bark and spotted Promise up on the stairs to the grandstand.

"What are you doing, Promise?" Wade yelled then whistled. "Come!"

Promise looked away. Her disobedience was a first.

"I said, get—" Wade saw what Promise was looking at.

Lacey.

She was on the top of the grandstand. He watched her slowly stand from her bench, and all Wade could do was shout, "Get down!" as he took off at full speed to reach her before flying bullets did.

Visions of sniper fire infiltrated his brain. Sand and

snow mixed together. Heat and cold shocked the system the same. Both slowed him down. He'd never make it.

"Promise! Cover Lacey!"

Wade's adrenaline kicked in, but still it would be Promise who would reach Lacey first. He saw his dog leap from bench to bench, gaining ground with every jump. Wade also saw the confusion on Lacey's face as he ran nearer. She had no idea there was a car on the other side of the track.

"Get down!" he yelled again right at the moment gunshots echoed over the track. Right at the moment Promise took her final and highest leap directly over Lacey, pushing her down.

Wade heard Lacey scream out, then her scream muffled to nothing. Had she been shot again?

"Lacey!" Wade called out, but stopped at the stairs to the grandstand. Making himself a target wouldn't help her. He had to get to her from behind. But that meant climbing up the joists of the grandstand. The last time he'd done that, people died. This time, Lacey would if he didn't. "Hang on! I'm coming!"

No answer.

Wade lunged for the first bar of the enormous bleachers. He swung to the next one, then the next. Beads of sweat burst from his forehead as his arms trembled with growing fatigue with each pull up to the top. He swung a leg up to the next bar and used his lower-body strength to carry him the rest of the way up.

Golden-red fur rustled in the wind above him, but that was all he could see moving. "Lacey? Are you all right?" He had to know before he reached her.

"Wade?" a faint muffled cry drifted to his ears.

"I'm right here." He reached out and touched the arm of his combat coat she wore. He'd made it to her side, but

he still needed to get her down off the bleachers. "I'm going to pull you down through the back. Are you hurt?"

"I don't think so. Promise pushed me down. It happened so fast, but, Wade..."

"What is it, Lacey? What's wrong?" he asked as he stabilized his feet in the rungs before he lifted her.

"I think...I think Promise is hurt. She's not moving, and she's breathing heavy. Oh, Wade, I don't know what I'll do if she's hurt. If she—"

"Shh, sweetheart. Promise is fine. She's just doing what I asked her to do. Cover you until I could get to you." Wade gave a low whistle. "Promise, stay low."

The dog shimmied down Lacey, and Wade got his first glimpse of Lacey's distraught face. She hadn't been worried about her own life but of his dog's.

"You're crazy, you know that? You get shot at, and you're worried about Promise. You're crazy, and I love... I love your beautiful heart." He dropped his forehead to hers as he put his arms under her.

Lacey reached for him with shaking arms. "How did they find us here?" Her voice trembled. "We made sure we weren't being followed."

"I don't know. They've got to be tracking us somehow. Come on, we have to move." Balancing on a rung, he tightened his hold on her. "It won't be long before they make it over here to see their handiwork. But, Lacey, we have to go down this way. We can't go down the stairs. We'll be seen and shot at again."

Lacey pulled back and turned her face.

"Don't look down," he said, but it was too late.

Her eyes widened in fright. "Oh, why did I have to pick the top bleacher to sit in?"

"Why did you get out of the car is what I want to know." Wade hoisted her around to his back. "Wrap

your arms around my neck but don't choke me, or we'll both go down." Wade let his body acclimate to the extra weight on him, but she really didn't weigh much more than his gear.

"I left because God didn't tell me no."

The muscles in Wade's arms twitched as he lowered down to the next rung. Her words pushed through the blood pulsing through his head from the exertion. "God didn't... Oh. We're back to that again? Do you see why your motto of going unless God tells you no might not be the best course of action? Once again, you put yourself in the line of fire."

"I'm sorry, but I thought after what happened in the car, you might have come this way. Oh, Wade, we are so high up."

Wade grunted as he brought them down to the next rung. "I told you not to look down." A quick look himself showed they had a ways to go. He focused on one rung at a time while he talked to keep her calm. "Why did you think I would be in the bleachers?"

She pressed her cheek to his so close he could feel her quick, nervous breaths against him. "Because of what happened here when you were eight. This is where you found the capsule, right? The place that man shook you for answers?"

Wade's chest tightened and his hands dampened with perspiration. "Don't go there, okay? Let's just get off this thing and get out of here." He looked down and his grip slipped. The bars released right from his hands.

In a split second they were free-falling. Wade frantically reached for another bar going by but missed.

Lacey screamed in his ear as they plummeted straight down, the air whooshing by them.

Wade made more quick-action grabs for the rungs fly-

ing by him. One hand made contact, but his sweaty grasp made it hard to hold on. He ground his teeth and pulled every ounce of body strength to stabilize his grasp even with only one hand.

They dangled in the air for long, heavy seconds. He focused on Lacey's hold around his neck. "Don't let go, Lacey."

"Wade?" she screeched in his ear. He didn't care. It meant she was still holding on.

He hadn't left her behind.

He swung his body back and forth until the momentum pushed him up to grab the bar with his free hanging hand. "No more talk of the past. We need to focus only on our current circumstances."

"But you can't if your past is still hurting you. And don't tell me it's not. I felt your pain in your kiss."

"Leave it be." Wade began the descent again.

Her arms tightened around his neck a little too much. "I can't leave it. God won't let me. He loves you and will never leave you."

The next rung came and went with his controlled and deliberate silence.

"You're not the only one with a plan, you know. God has one, too, and you can't stop His plan, no matter how much you strategize. He's pursuing you because He wants you to belong to Him."

"You're choking me," Wade said.

"Choking you? I'm telling you the truth. You have nothing to fear from Him. He wants to show you that you're worth His love. Believe it, and it will help you with your pain and healing."

"Not if you kill me first," he struggled to say. "You're choking me." With his feet secure on a rung, he risked

letting one hand loose to tap her arms where they were so tight around his neck he could no longer breathe.

"Oh! I'm so sorry. I thought you meant…well, you know what I thought." She released the pressure, but her talk of God and love still had a way of stanching the flow of air to his lungs. His foot touched ground and not a moment too soon.

"Get to the car. I'm driving!" he commanded as he bent his legs to allow Lacey to lower herself from his back. He saw his dog already waited for him at the bottom. "To the car, Promise."

The dog took off ahead of them. Lacey ran ahead as well, around the old delivery truck and through the snow. They reached the car and jumped in at the same time. Promise took up her post on the passenger-side floor, watching both of them with her familiar curiosity. Her eyebrows bounced up and down as she made her assessment of the situation, or at least of him.

"I'm okay, Promise," he said as the car roared to life. He spun it out of the parking lot in a quick squealing turn.

Wade checked his mirrors and found darkness around him.

Lacey craned her neck to see behind her. "We can't go to the house. We'll only lead more danger to Roni."

"You're right. We'll go to Clay's. He's right in town, with lots of neighbors and a security gate. He'll know what the best course of action is. I trust him completely."

TWELVE

Clay's sprawling pristine Victorian sat eminently on top of Norcastle's highest hill as though it were Camelot itself. Wade pulled up to a black iron gate and punched a code to slide the bars open—bars that had the initials C.S. at the gate's center. A little pretentious, Lacey thought. Even if the crime rate warranted such security measures for a gate, she had to think the initials were a little much.

"Are there a lot of break-ins around here?" she asked when Wade paused for the gate to close behind them.

"I'm not here enough to know, but if Clay feels safer, I won't judge. And if the break-in at the speedway is a regular event, then your answer would be yes."

Wade had told her about the ransacked office at the track. There was definitely crime to contend with in this still struggling town, racetrack or no. Plus, Lacey wouldn't deny the fact that she felt safer already being on the inside of those gates, however pompous the initials were.

Wade took the long, curved driveway, lined with ornate black lantern posts, up and around the hill until the car pulled into a wide parking area with a six-bay garage.

She felt her lips curve uncontrollably. "Something tells me there are some powerful horses behind those doors. And I don't mean of the equine variety."

"Do you ever think of anything else besides cars?" Wade asked.

"Do you ever think about anything else besides plans?"

"I'd say my plans have kept you alive so far."

Lacey conceded. "You're right. Your plans really worked when those bullets have flown at me this week. Thank you."

"A good military plan is one that stays together after the bullets fly. So let's try to avoid another go-round, shall we?" Wade's lips broke into a small smile. "Stay with me."

They opened the doors and climbed out, heading to the stone steps at the back entrance.

The house was a real showplace. Clay hadn't spared any expense in making it magazine worthy. Lacey could picture the man who liked a good party, as he had told her, hosting many of them here. But Lacey supposed the owner of a prosperous business would need a place like this for hosting hospitality events.

Except he wasn't really the owner of the business, was he?

Lacey knew he was filling in until Wade was ready to take over his responsibilities. She also knew Clay wasn't rushing Wade to step up the way Roni was, and Roni didn't like Clay for it.

Was there anything else she didn't like him for?

Wade paused to look down the driveway. Did a noise catch his ear? Or was it someone?

Had they been tracked down again? So soon? How had they gotten inside the gate?

Lacey's heart jumped into her throat as she awaited word from him. She breathed easier when he began walking again.

Promise whined from where she trotted along at their feet.

Lacey rubbed her fingers through the dog's fur to soothe her. "It's all right, Promise. Don't you worry." Lacey looked over at Wade. "Right?"

Wade whispered, "I don't know how long we can stay here. It doesn't look as if Clay's home."

"So why can't we stay? Would it upset him that we're in his home?"

"Negative."

"*Negative?* You're always so formal when you're in your army mode. You sound like an instructional manual. And, yes, before you say it, I have read instructional manuals before. I don't always wing it." She turned to see him not even listening to her, his face etched like stone as he concentrated on something unknown to her. She followed the direction of his gaze into the thick dark trees at the rear of the property. "Wade, you're scaring me. What is it?"

He didn't answer but ushered her up the walkway and steps a little faster. At the back door, Wade found the spare key and opened the house with ease. He guided her in and said, "Get down."

Having been shot at so much this week, Lacey didn't argue. She found herself facedown on a thick Oriental rug of red-and-purple paisley. Gold flecks burst from the print as well as a myriad of other colors she wouldn't have picked up if she'd stayed on her feet like Wade.

He walked from window to window pulling curtains and drawing shades, moving on to the next room.

Lacey elbow crawled to a place she could see him traverse to the next room after that, then disappear around another corner.

Minutes went by from her prostrate position. "Wade?"

she called with uncertainty in her voice. "Can you tell me what's going on?"

"I'd like to know that, too," a male's voice spoke from behind her, extracting the air straight from her lungs.

Lacey spun around and pushed up to a sitting position, crab crawling back a few feet from two men towering over her.

Recognition filtered in when one of them spoke. "We meet again, Lacey."

It was Wade's Uncle Clay. He didn't look as good as he had when she first met him. His hair seemed a bit disheveled. His fancy clothes had been replaced by jeans with dirt on the knees. Being so low to the floor, she couldn't miss them. The dirt didn't compute with the owner of this opulent house.

Even so, she sighed and her shoulders sagged. "It's just you. You scared me. Wade, your uncle's home! He's got company with him!"

Clay stepped by her and peered through to the next room. "This is my friend Chuck Teigen. Chuck, this is the girl I told you about. Her brother was the one who just passed."

Lacey looked up to find a hand offered to her. The man behind it was tall with white hair, but a bit younger than Clay. She accepted his handshake. "Nice to meet you."

"Likewise. I'm sorry about the loss of your brother."

"Thank you." Lacey felt the familiar lump in her throat threatening to take hold when Jeff's face appeared in her mind.

"May I ask why you're on the floor?" the man asked.

The present circumstances snapped her back to reality. "Wade wanted me to stay down until he secured the house. The bullets haven't stopped flying at me since Christmas Eve."

Clay took a seat against the side wall. His hands curled around the armrests of a Queen Anne chair. His eyes that had been so cheerful at Christmas now sharpened on her. "I'm glad to see you're all right. We've been beside ourselves with worry. Especially when we didn't hear from either of you after the thugs obliterated the garage."

"I'm sorry we couldn't call. We had to lose any device we might be tracked by, including the phones and Wade's GPS watch."

"That's what we figured. I told Roni to stop worrying."

"Roni! She most likely will have some visitors tonight. We have to get a message to her to stay inside."

"She's not home. I've been out there cleaning up the place, but she and Cora have been staying with Cora's sister since you two left. Roni's still really shaken up."

Lacey knew firsthand what it felt like not to know if your brother was alive or dead. "Not knowing where Wade is must be killing her."

"Both of us," Clay said. "But I have some friends at the government level who have been looking into the attack on Christmas Eve and trying to track you guys down."

"One of your lawyers, politicians or PIs you told me about?" She remembered his words to her on Christmas when he'd offered to help her uncover the truth of her brother's death.

Clay nodded to the other man still standing. "Chuck is one of them. Or, as the public knows him, Senator Charles Teigen."

"Senator?" Lacey frowned and mumbled as she raised her head higher to the man still towering over her. "Now I feel really silly for sitting on the floor."

Senator Teigen smiled down at her. His hazel eyes shined. "Don't feel silly. Wade's a smart tactical military

man. If he says it's safer for you, then you would be wise to follow his orders."

Guilt niggled in. "I'm sorry to say I haven't exactly been a good follower. I know I've made things a lot harder for him because of it."

"I can't believe my ears," a familiar voice spoke from behind. "Are you finally understanding the error of your ways?"

Instantly, the air in the room charged with a bolt of electricity as Wade walked in with a laptop tucked under one arm and a duffel bag over his shoulder.

Lacey jumped to her feet. "Exactly what error are you talking about?"

Wade frowned and pointed at the window. "*That* error. You just jumped up in front of a window. Granted, the curtain's closed, but you didn't even look before you stood. Your split-second decisions are going to get you killed."

"All right, Wade, go easy on her." Clay stood and offered Lacey his chair out of the line of the many windows. "As much as I should teach my nephew a few lessons in decorum, right now I just want to hug him."

Clay walked over to Wade and reached for him. Wade dropped the bag to the floor to return the half embrace, the laptop still under his other arm. Lacey could only see Clay's back when he asked, "Are you okay, son?" but something in the way he asked this simple question spoke volumes. Wade's small family understood his pain. They worried about his state of mind, but most important, they loved him.

And by staying away from them, Wade rejected their love, too.

Lacey averted her gaze through the doorway into the dining room behind the men. The senator was on his

cell phone letting someone know she and Wade were safe. This was one of the men Clay mentioned to her who might be able to help her figure out what had happened to Jeff.

Lacey left Wade and his uncle to approach the senator. "Sir? Do you have a moment?"

"The police are on their way." The man pocketed his phone and offered a warm smile. "How can I help you?"

"Clay mentioned you might be able to look into my brother's death." She knew she'd blurted it out, but there was no other way to say it.

The man slowly nodded. "Yes, he did ask me to put some people on it. Especially after the shooting. We can only assume the incidents are related."

"And?" Did she dare hope Senator Teigen would help her find the truth when so many had given her the same excuse for Jeff's death? That it was an accident?

"And, Miss Phillips, I think we need to talk. I believe your reservations are well founded, and I'm of the mind that there's more to this case than what has been documented."

Lacey's knees wobbled as hope blossomed. She reached for his hand. "Thank you, sir."

"You're quite welcome, but honestly, if something is amiss in the military, I would want to find out, regardless if you asked me to or not."

Lacey smiled at the man, feeling as if her path had led her to this place tonight, no matter how dangerous it had been.

Senator Teigen reached into his inside coat pocket and removed a business card. "Let's get through tonight, and we'll chat in the morning. My private number is on there."

Lacey looked at the card, excitement rushing through her. She wished it was already morning.

"Why didn't you ever tell me my parents were divorced?" Wade's angry voice broke her bubble. She placed the card in Wade's combat jacket's bottom pocket and followed Senator Teigen to the other room.

"Is there a problem, gentlemen?" he asked.

Wade waved a hand to the laptop on the mahogany sideboard, now open and running. The divorce document appeared on the screen.

Clay's blanched face was filled with sorrow. He cast a glance Lacey's way before returning to Wade with a disappointed sigh. "I never saw the need to cause you more pain. Besides, the divorce never went through. They were still married when they died, and as far as I was concerned, things looked as if they would stay that way even before the accident. Whatever it was that set the proceeding in motion rectified itself. One day, my brother was distraught and brokenhearted. The next, he was overjoyed, and the divorce was off. A week later, they both died in the accident, and I'm presented with two orphaned children to raise." Clay blinked his eyes, then pinched the bridge of his nose. "Look, I did what I thought was best for you and Veronica. I never saw any reason to ruin your memory of your parents. Please tell me you understand. I don't think I could take you hating me, too. Veronica's feelings toward me have been painful enough."

Wade's anger transferred onto Roni. "I'm sorry about her. All I can think is she's angry at me for leaving, and she's taking it out on you. She doesn't understand that you're helping me more than her guilt trips to come home do."

"I know, and that's what I've said to her, but… Oh, well, she's Roni. There's no one like her in this world. She has her ideas of what's important and nothing you

can say will change her mind. Her drum is already beating to a rhythm none of us can ever march correctly to, in her opinion. As far as I'm concerned, she'll end up alone because men are afraid to ask her to dance. They know they won't be the one leading."

Lacey cleared her throat to tell them she was still in the room. "Can we look at the pictures? I want to see them again."

"What pictures?" Clay asked.

Wade clicked on the file with the newspaper clippings. He scrolled through one by one.

Clay stepped closer. "My, oh, my, don't these bring back memories. Yes, that one there was from the ribbon-cutting ceremony at Spencer Speedway. The whole town was there. Well, practically anyway. Not everyone was excited about a racetrack opening in their quiet mountain town."

Lacey queued into the conversation. "Like who?"

"Oh, just a few people who I think didn't want a lot of strangers in town. One of them used to live in this house, actually. Eventually put the house up for sale and moved out. Worked out well for me." Clay flashed a smile and a wink. "He realized he could try to make a lot of noise, but those cars made a lot more. And so did the people who hadn't had work for many years."

Lacey zeroed in on the button pinned to the man in the background. "Is that what that button is about? It says, Vote for Jobs."

"Exactly. There had to be a town vote to allow the track to open. It won by a landslide. That's Meredith's father, Gary Shelton, in the picture. He really pushed for the vote to pass. Chuck helped out, too, at the state level. Right, Chuck?"

"Sure did. The track has been good for the whole state's economy."

Lacey smiled at the man. Knowing a senator didn't hurt. She looked back at the picture. "Where is Meredith's father now?"

Wade cut in to answer, "My grandfather died of a heart attack shortly after my parents. I didn't know him well. Obviously couldn't even recognize him in the photo, even if it wasn't grainy. He seemed to show up only when another baby was born. The last time I saw him was when Luke was born, eighteen months prior."

Lacey frowned, thinking of that small child in the fire with them all. Such a horrific thing to happen. She looked at Wade and felt for him more, knowing he lived with that nightmare every day, more so than Roni, even. She'd been three years old and didn't remember much, but Wade had been old enough to remember every horrid detail. Especially the detail of having to leave that infant behind.

No wonder he never wanted to leave another person behind. Lacey had to think this made him a good captain in the army, but just how many deaths could a person grieve?

Clay chuckled. "I always thought your grandfather was part of the mafia or something. He had so much money, and to this day, I still don't know what he did. If I asked Meredith, she always said he's into a little of this and a little of that. Always so vague."

"Are we even sure the man was her father?" Wade asked.

Clay's eyes squinted. "I'm not following. You think she lied about who her father was? What would be the point?"

Wade looked at Lacey for a few beats. Was he wait-

ing for her to give him some direction? How much he divulged was totally up to him. Especially when he believed people died when he talked. This was more than a simple dilemma of whether or not to share a family secret. This was a death sentence to anyone he spoke to.

But not for her.

"Clay—" Lacey spoke for Wade "—we think Meredith might have been involved in some illegal activity. We think she might have been a spy, possibly working with the Russians. Wade is trying to put the pieces together, and that means questioning all he believed to be true. If this man wasn't the 'bouncing on your knee' kind of granddaddy, it would stand to reason he might not have been a grandfather at all, but a boss of some kind. Perhaps her handler."

Quizzical silence ensued from Clay. He looked at Senator Teigen, standing by quietly. "Chuck, maybe you should step out."

"Of course." The senator turned to give them privacy, but Lacey stopped him.

"Please stay. If you're going to help, you'll need to know all the details." She directed everyone's attention back to the screen. "Jeffrey was helping Wade investigate." She nodded to the computer. "This was all his research. He found the divorce papers and these newspaper clippings. It seems he was also collecting his evidence and writing a book called *A Russian Spy at an American Racetrack*, so that might be what contributed to his death, if the wrong person found out. But regardless, we are now dodging bullets, and Wade really doesn't want to add any more targets for them to aim at."

"I see."

"Do you, Clay?" Wade asked. "Because by us being here we have put you in harm's way."

"Don't you worry about me, son. I'm just torn to shreds that you have lived with this alone for so long. How long have you known, exactly?"

"I found some incriminating evidence when I was eighteen in one of Mom's secret rooms. I left shortly after for the army."

"That long? Man, Wade, I wish you would have come to me then. You know I would have helped you put this together if that's what you wanted."

"I couldn't. I was still too scared from when I told a man under the grandstand something my mother didn't want known. Four hours later, she and Dad and Luke were dead. I couldn't lose another family member."

"Wade, your parents' death was an accident. You can't blame yourself for that day."

"But what if it wasn't an accident? What if someone killed them?"

"I'd say you're talking nonsense, but I will say if Meredith was involved in criminal activity, it would be grounds for divorce. Bobby never told me why he was filing. He just said he had to. Now I see why."

"Dad must have found out his wife was into something illegal and dangerous."

"So then, what changed his mind about the divorce?" Lacey asked.

"Or rather, who?" Clay said.

"What do you mean?" Lacey and Wade asked simultaneously.

Clay walked to the window and lifted the curtain's edge. He peered out into the darkness for a minute before dropping it back into place. He stepped back to his chair and slouched down in it. "You mentioned that you hadn't seen your grandfather since Luke's birth, but you're wrong. He came for a quick visit a week before

they died. When I say quick, I mean it. Like less than an hour. I took you kids out for some ice cream. When I got back he was gone, and the divorce was off. Whatever he'd said to them changed Bobby's mind."

"Or whatever he'd threatened did," Wade said.

Promise let out a loud bark and ran to the window Clay had just looked out.

"Promise, sit and shush," Wade instructed.

Lacey knelt from where she stood and called Promise to come to her. "Wade, she barely ever barks unless she has a reason to. She's upset about some—"

Lacey never finished her sentence because blasts came through the window, blowing the curtain up to the ceiling and spraying glass all over the room. Bullets lodged in the wall, right behind the spot Lacey had been standing in before she knelt to call Promise.

She threw herself flat to the floor, stunned, as the other three men followed her down, as well.

They'd been found again. And the gate had failed to keep them safe.

Wade crawled across the floor toward Lacey. She grabbed hold of his reaching arms and pulled her belly across the floor to meet him.

"Were you hit?" he asked, pressed against her ear. His voice cracked and all she could do was look at the hole in the wall and shake her head. Her throat was so tight with fear no words could be formed, just moving lips of silence.

Her fingers pressed deep into his back as Wade pressed his cheek against hers. "I don't know how much more I can take of this, Lacey. It's getting harder every time watching you go down because of me. This has to end. Right now." Abruptly, Wade jumped to his feet, leaving her grasping for him in the cold, vacant place he left

behind. “Stay down,” he commanded as he drew his gun and lurched right through the hanging drape and out the busted-open window.

A gun exploded into the night from behind the curtain. The image of the bullet finding Wade and killing him had Lacey finally finding her voice. “No!”

THIRTEEN

A bullet whizzed past the top of Wade's head and hit the brick chimney behind him. Stone and mortar crumbled down on him. He dared not move from his crouched place in the hedge, not even to brush away the brick pieces from his shoulders. With arms outstretched, gun cocked and ready, Wade surveyed the scene for his next move. Running out blind would only get him killed.

The barking of the neighbors' dogs wasn't helping his focus. Deep howls and high-pitched yaps sang in a canine chorus up and down the street. The gunman probably hadn't thought about what shooting off a round of bullets would do in a small town. Out on the mountaintop nobody heard a thing, but in the village of Norcastle, people would be nosy. Wade gave it another sixty seconds before he heard sirens. That meant he had less than that to catch this guy before he disappeared into the moonless night.

Wade scanned the tree line. When he and Lacey had arrived at Clay's house, Wade had thought he'd heard something rustling in the trees. He'd chalked it up to a breeze. After all, how could anyone get past the gate, and how could they know they were here in the first place?

Simple, Wade thought. They still had a trace on them.

He didn't know how, but the gunman was going to squawk—right after Wade tracked him down.

The hedge to his right was eight feet away. He would probably be able to make it, but the move was too logical. The guy would be expecting him to make the attempt to reach it for cover. Wade needed another strategy, one less obvious.

Wade looked to his left. Jeff's spotting commands to Lacey to go left flashed in his mind. But it was twelve feet of open space to the corner of the house where the porch jutted out and rounded to the front. The small bushes there wouldn't be enough to hide behind. Going left didn't appear to be an option. Then he spotted another alternative.

A large metal shovel leaned against the porch. Clay's snow-removal service must have left it there when they shoveled the walk last. Didn't matter, Wade thought. The thing screamed metal shield. Just what he needed to cover him, *if* he could make it to the porch to grab it.

He didn't wait for a count but made the dash. Just as expected, bullets spattered against the house in a trail behind him. He took the last five feet in the air with a vertical leap, grabbing the handle of the shovel as he flew by it.

Wade landed and rolled back on his feet with the shovel upside down in front of his chest and face. He ran right for the trees, the direction the bullets had come from, a bonus of allowing the guy to get off a few shots. Now Wade knew where to run.

In an unpredictable zigzag motion, Wade raced forward and spotted the guy heading downhill. A car's engine started up off in the distance somewhere beyond the gate. He kept his eye on the gunman and soon was close enough to lose the shovel. With his empty hand he

grabbed the back collar of a heavyset man, tackled him to the ground and disarmed him.

Wade had him on his back with the gun to his head just as sirens filled the night.

Sixty seconds, just as he'd thought.

The car he'd heard start a few seconds ago spun off from its hiding place below.

"Looks as if your getaway got away without you," Wade said to the angry face below him. It was the same man from the train station, the same one who had grabbed Lacey. "You're all alone with no one to help you now, Pudgy. I suggest you start talking. Perhaps the law will go easy on you if you do. All I want to know is who you work for."

The guy slammed his head into Wade's. Eye-blinding pain radiated out from Wade's head, but he held fast. He rammed his forearm under the man's chin to hold him down but quickly noticed white foam bubbling out of the man's mouth. The gurgling sounds and the way the man's black eyes widened and rolled to the back of his head told Wade the man just took his own life.

Wade jumped off him in confusion and shock. The guy must have had some sort of pill lodged in his mouth. When he'd butted his forehead, the impact had dislodged it so he could ingest it.

Wade flipped the guy over. "Spit it out!" he yelled. "Nothing is worth this. Not even your boss. Your life is worth more than this."

Police cars screamed up the hill to the house, but Wade barely registered their approach. He hadn't even heard the gates open in his frenzy to shake the pill from the man's mouth. Clay must have opened them from inside.

Wade released the dead man and rolled onto his back with his forearm over his eyes. He pushed hard to try to

erase the image, as if that ever worked. How many times would he have to watch another death?

When an officer appeared above him, Wade sat up but pushed him off.

"Wade, is that you?" It was a woman officer. She shone her flashlight on him. "What's going on here? More shooting?"

Wade opened his eyes and found Chief Sylvie Laurent crouched down by the dead body, her blond hair pulled tight into a bun. She and Wade had gone to school together but Wade barely knew her. Sylvie had grown up literally on the other side of the tracks. Not that Wade would ever let that determine who his friends were. The fact was, Wade had chosen to be a loner for other reasons than money. But he was pretty sure Sylvie didn't know that. She probably figured Wade was the rich snob her family worked for at the track who was too good for them. Little did she know he envied her family the few times he saw them working together. Her brother raced; she was part of his pit crew. Even her son helped out on race days. Wade figured she would be the first to say the racetrack had given her the courage to go after the chief of police job. Wade thought that under different circumstances, Lacey would have gotten along well with Norcastle's chief.

Chief Laurent reached for the dead guy's neck to take a pulse.

"Don't bother," Wade said. "He's dead.

"I see that. Did you shoot him?"

"Nope. You won't find a bullet hole on him anywhere. At least not a fresh one. He took his own life. Had some sort of capsule ready to do the deed if I should catch him trying to take us out. It would appear the guy's reality scared him more than death." Wade pushed to his feet

and looked down at the man who gave nothing about that reality away. Not even a name. "He wasn't working alone. He was sent to kill us, but I have no idea by whom."

Paramedics and police stepped in to evaluate the body and begin to process the scene. Their night had just become a long one. Wade didn't envy them, but that didn't mean he meant to stay out here another second.

A glance at the busted window showed curtains blowing a little from the cold wind. Behind them Lacey waited for word.

She waited for him.

Somehow, the idea brought him comfort, and his feet moved toward her faster.

"Where you going, Spencer?" the chief called out.

"I need to tell everyone it's all clear," Wade replied without a backward glance.

The pull to be near Lacey in this moment was stronger than any pull he'd ever felt. Maybe it was because another person had died in front of him. Maybe he knew she was frightened, and he wanted to ease her fear. Either of those responses would be legit. But deep down, Wade knew he wanted to be near her for completely selfish reasons. He wanted her in his arms. He wanted to feel her heartbeat against him. He wanted the vibrant evidence of life she exemplified in everything crazy and impulsive she did. Lacey in his arms, where she was safe and sound, where he could breathe her in and fill himself with everything she was, suddenly became the most important thing in the world to him.

Wade walked to the broken window, but his racing heart wouldn't allow him to speak. The drape still hung, blocking his view to the inside. Would she still be down as he had commanded? Probably not, he thought, and

his trembling lips curled in a smile at the idea of Lacey ever following orders.

Wade forced his lips to form a whistle so he could alert Promise to come to the window, but before he made a sound, he heard Lacey speak.

"I should go home," she said.

The words knocked the whistle out of Wade. Yes, it was what he had been saying to her from the beginning. Yes, it was the smart thing for her to do. And yes, he wanted her safe.

But...

But nothing. It was for the best that she did go home. He had nothing to offer her but a life of pain. If he really wanted her safe, then she had no business being near him.

Finally, the girl was making sense. She should go home.

So why did this idea cut him down faster than the car that took down his family?

But then, what was one more pain anyway?

"I should go home?" Lacey said again, trying to wrap her mind around Clay's suggestion.

"Yes, Lacey, you should." Clay reached to rub Promise's head.

Promise grumbled and moved closer to Lacey, where she sat on the floor in the same place she'd gone down at the first gunshots. Even when more shots went off, and all she wanted to do was run out after Wade, she stayed put. Going after him would make his job harder if he had to protect her at the same time he apprehended the gunman. And he *would* apprehend the man. She had to believe that.

The sirens had sounded like music to her ears. Senator

Teigen had already called the police before, but a neighbor or two must have heard the shots and called, as well.

Promise growled again and Lacey reached to pet her. "She must want to be with Wade to help him. She's not normally like this. She's usually so sweet."

Clay guffawed. "Sweet? She's a military dog. Trained to kill if she's commanded to. I wouldn't call her sweet."

"Kill? Promise? No, she's a service animal. She's trained to be gentle and attentive, to assist her soldier in everyday life skills. She can flip light switches and wake him from nightmares. She can even bring Wade his shoes, if need be. She's so good for him, and speaking of him, where is he? He should be coming back in for us. Do you think he was hurt? Maybe we should go out there."

"I'm sure the police need his help right now. He's also trained to kill and will know what to do with this gunman. That's why I really think you need to go home. You're a good girl, Lacey. I would hate to see you get hurt in all this mess."

"Going home will make me feel as if I'm bailing on Wade. My brother already bailed on him. I don't want to, also. I want to help him."

"Do you love him? Is that what this is about? You're setting yourself up for a world of hurt, if that's the case. Wade's incapable of loving you back."

"I don't love him," Lacey said with a little too much force, even to her own ears.

"Good." Wade interrupted the conversation as he stepped into the room. "Keep it that way."

He bypassed her on the floor and went straight to the laptop, pushing Senator Teigen out of the way. Slowly she got to her feet to see him downloading the files from the USB to the laptop. When they'd been copied over,

he disengaged the USB drive, turned the butt of his gun over and smashed the drive to pieces.

"What are you doing?" Lacey raced to his side. "That's Jeff's!"

"Exactly. I should never have trusted your brother in the first place. He turned on me, and now I've got criminals showing up in places trying to take us out. They're tracking us somehow. It can't be our phones, and it can't be my watch. What else is there but the USB drive your brother, *the traitor*, created."

Lacey locked eyes on the tiny pieces. Guilt filled her because of her brother's actions. "I'm sorry."

"It's not your offense to be sorry for, but it is the one you're paying for. You should be just as angry with him." Wade slammed the laptop cover down and lifted it under his arm. "The police need to see the files, and they'll help you get home. This trek together is over." Wade turned his back on her and lifted his duffel bag. "Clay, can I take your Lexus when I leave? I have some things I want to check out, and I can't take Jeff's car. Who knows if he installed a tracker on that, too."

"You don't want any of my cars, then. All of mine have locaters on them."

"Right." Wade gave a whistle and Promise sidled up beside him. The two walked toward the exit, side by side.

"I thought you said you would never leave another person behind?" she shouted just as the door opened. Wade paused on the threshold.

"I'm leaving you where you're safe. That's different." With that, Wade walked through, closing the door behind him.

Lacey took off to chase him down. Clay reached a hand to stop her, but she shook it off. She would not be left behind. Down the steps and past Clay's black Lexus

Sport, she ran straight into the teams of authorities processing the scene. She saw Wade with the laptop open, sharing the files with a few plainclothes detectives.

Then Lacey noticed the cloth covering a mound on the grass. Only that wasn't a mound. It was a body.

The gunman was dead? Why hadn't Wade told them?

A wave of nausea rolled through Lacey's stomach. She studied Wade's profile in the laptop lighting and knew what this meant.

He'd killed the man.

Her steps slowed as she passed the body. Bile rose in her throat. Knowing the act was a matter of self-defense didn't make accepting it any easier. She looked at Wade and wondered what would this do to him. He claimed to cherish life, even though Clay said Wade was trained to kill. Lacey didn't believe for a second that each death didn't affect him. No death was inconsequential, no matter whose side they were on.

Which meant this death would be another injury to Wade's already wounded mind and body.

"It's not your fault," she said from her place by the deceased. The detectives and Wade stopped their discussion and looked at her over the screen. "It's not your fault. You did what you had to do to protect innocent people." She stepped up to him, her eyes locked on his. She hoped no judgment or fear shone out at him. *God, stay with me while I give him Your grace.* "None of them were your fault, Wade. None of them."

Wade's eyes glistened in the laptop light reflecting on his face; his dimple deepened and twitched. But he didn't look away from her. "It doesn't change the fact that I will always see them dead in my mind. Broken necks, missing parts, hollow eyes. It doesn't matter whose fault it was. Like this guy." He nodded to the man on the ground. "He

took his own life, Lacey. Right in front of me, so I will have to remember him dead forever."

"He took his own life?" The shock at this fact was nothing compared to the shock Wade must have had watching it. "Oh, Wade." She ran straight at him. He had to quickly pass the laptop off to one of the men so his arms were ready for her. She pushed hard into him, pressed her arms around his back, her head into his neck. Soon dampness covered her face from her tears. She offered him compassion for his pain. She wished she could offer him so much more. She held on tight and refused to let go. She didn't care if he rejected it all, she would keep dishing it out.

But something happened she least expected.

Wade hugged her back.

At first it was the slow rise of his arms around her, but soon he pressed into her and held on, too.

A long time went by before they lifted wet faces and stared at each other. The detectives had stepped away, giving them privacy, but no words came from Wade's and Lacey's lips. Their gazes spoke for them. No judgment, just gratitude, but there were also a few questions on trust.

Both of them had their blinders off and knew the other person could hurt them more than anyone in this world.

But they also knew which one of them would cause the other the most pain, however unintentional. Slowly, Wade dropped his arms and stepped back. "I don't want to hurt you," he whispered.

Lacey looked beyond his shoulder, feeling what his rejection would be like already. "I don't want you to hurt me, either."

"I can't promise you that it would never happen. In fact, I can promise you that it will. I can't be the person

you deserve and who deserves your love. I'd never live up to it."

Lacey nodded, but inside she screamed at herself. She'd thought she would be strong enough to handle his rejection. To prove to him she was strong enough. But instead, he'd proved to her that she wasn't.

Heavy moments passed and her blurred gaze fell to the laptop screen the detectives were studying. The letters from the soda-pop delivery truck were enlarged, and when she blinked they came into focus from her spot.

With her eyes on the screen, she noticed not all the letters from the truck were photographed; only certain letters were captured.

D—P—R—O—A—E—D—D

Lacey's mind started to sound out the word it made, only it wasn't anything intelligible. It was just a collection of random letters. Or was it?

Quickly, she swapped letters around and came up with the word *dead* something.

She nodded to the screen. "Wade, look. I'm not positive, but I think the letters Jeff took pictures of are supposed to say something."

Wade turned to give his attention to the screen. "Like what?"

"I don't know. He took a lot of pictures of this truck, though. It was important, I think. I see the word *dead.* Maybe something dead?"

Wade reached the detectives and grabbed the laptop from their hands. He studied it, then slammed the cover shut. "I need a ride to the track. Can either one of you take me?" he asked the detectives. At their agreement of which one would go, they headed to an unmarked car.

"What about me?" Lacey followed on his heels.

"You're to stay with my uncle, where it's safe."

"Safe? I don't live like that. Don't you know that by now? I take risks, Wade, even when I'm afraid." Her words meant much more than going in the car with him now. They really meant, *Take a chance on me in your life.*

"Stay, Lacey."

"I'm not your dog, Wade. You can't command me like you do Promise."

Promise followed along, her ears perked up at her name. Wade opened the back door of the car and she leaped in before him.

With one of Wade's legs inside, Lacey stopped him and said, "Let me help you. That's all I want from you."

"And then you'll go home?" His eyes pierced her as sharp as his request.

Lacey frowned. She dropped her shoulders in defeat and nodded. "If that's what you want from me."

Wade stepped out of the car. "Get in." He waved a hand for her to climb in first.

Lacey slid over to the far side to allow space for Wade. Promise put her paws on Lacey's lap and licked her face, excited about the car ride. Only this ride, with Wade's decision about their future made, felt far from a joyride.

"Back to the track," Wade told the detective driving them. "Lacey's right. The letters are a message. They say, *dead drop.* My mother must have been using the truck as her means to pass intelligence, and Jeff figured it out."

FOURTEEN

Silence mixed with the low whistle of the wind blowing over the track. Snow swirled along the ground and their feet as they trekked toward the old truck. Wade split his attention between the truck and his surroundings, tuning in for any sounds or movement that told him they weren't alone.

The detective went to the broken-in office to assess that scene and determine its correlation to the events of the evening.

"Wade, I know you probably don't want to hear this, but I'm beginning to think my brother didn't betray you."

"He was writing a book, Lacey."

"Or making it look like he was, in case someone found the USB drive."

"We had a plan. He was supposed to put everything in the locker. He didn't. End of story."

"Maybe everything happened so fast he didn't have time to get it there. Or maybe he knew how you felt about digressing from the plan, so he made his own on the side just in case."

"Why are you doing this now, Lacey?"

"Because I feel as if we're being guided right now. I feel as if I've got my earbud in my ear and my spotter

standing above taking the whole course in. I feel every step I take is protected and sure."

"And you think it's Jeff?"

"Jeff and God."

"Well, let's get looking and find out, but stay by my side." Wade grabbed Lacey's hand and pulled her around the back of the truck. A flimsy rusted lock secured the doors. It took one whack with the butt of his gun to break the metal in two. He worked the handle until it turned and opened the two doors on a loud echoing creak.

The interior of the delivery truck stood empty but for some hanging cobwebs. Lacey climbed in to feel the cold, dark corners for anything.

Nothing but an empty truck.

"I'm going through to the front driver's seat," Lacey told him, and disappeared through the small opening to the front of the truck. "Come around to the passenger side. I'll unlock it from the inside and let you in."

Before Wade moved, he heard a crunch very similar to a car tire in hardened snow. Thinking it came from the track, he moved around the side of the truck toward it. The front driver's-side door opened and Lacey poked her head out.

"I don't see anything up here, either. The truck's empty. Nothing under the seats, nothing in the glove box. I guess I was wrong. We weren't being guided here by Jeff or God. Hey, earth to Wade, are you listening to me?"

He put his fingers to his lips, and Lacey took the hint.

He reached the driver's door, an ear still tuned for any more sounds. A search for the detective through the truck's windows came up empty. The view to the office was blocked. "If only this truck worked," Wade thought aloud. "We could drive it out of here."

"How do you know it doesn't? Maybe I can hotwire it." She got down on the truck's floor.

"No time, Lacey. And I doubt there's any gas left in it, if the engine even worked. Let's get out of here."

Only when he reached for her, Lacey's eyes were so wide, he halted.

"What is it? What's wrong?"

She brought her hand out from under the dash, and in her palm was a black capsule. The surprise on her face had to match his own. "Does this look familiar?"

Wade couldn't breathe. It was the thing that had set everything in motion that long-ago day when he'd found it stashed in the grandstand. The whole world ceased to turn in his mind as he stared at the container that had begun it all. All the secrets and all the deaths.

"Put it back." The words spilled from his mouth. When she didn't move, he shouted, "I said, put it back! Whatever that is, it's deadly, and I don't want it anywhere near you."

The passenger door behind Lacey swung wide. A man in a black suit reached in and pulled Lacey out from her waist. He had a gun to her head before Wade could engage. Wade pulled his own gun from the back of his waistband, but immediately felt a hand from behind, snatching it away. Wade whipped around to meet a gun pointed at his chest. He looked up at the face that the gun belonged to.

No recognition at all. Just another man in a high-end suit. This one clean-cut like…military.

From the other side of the truck, Promise barked more ferociously than Wade had ever heard her bark before. For her to bark like that, things had to be going down fast over there. Lacey yelled, "Put me down!" She continued to scream into the night. Then her voice muffled as though someone had covered her mouth.

Wade could spit nails. "Tell your man to leave her alone. This doesn't involve her."

"We'll decide that. And it's men. You're outnumbered, eight to three. Four, if I give you the dog." The guy pointed his gun at the center of Wade's chest and invited him to look and see.

One glance and Wade saw the red dot locked on him.

"The cop and your girlfriend are wearing one, too. What's your decision?"

An image of Lacey and the detective lying in a pool of their own blood, staining the white snow, filled Wade's mind. He didn't even have to see the deaths and they were already imprinted on his brain. More deaths to live with. But Lacey's? No, not Lacey's.

Wade's breathing picked up. He gnashed his teeth in frustration. Hearing her cries just added to the sour sickness in his stomach. What were they doing to her? What could he do for her? Nothing. "Who are you and what do you want?"

"Walk slowly around the truck and get in the car."

"We're not going anywhere with you."

The gun clicked, but Wade held every eyelash in place. He could disarm the guy. He knew how.

But the risk was too great. Wade sneered at the man and skirted the truck, his choices limited…for now.

The sight around the truck nearly undid him. Two men held Lacey by the arms while another one held a gun on her. The detective was apprehended facedown in the snow, disarmed by two men. Promise growled and bit into the pant leg of one of the men holding Lacey.

The gun in Wade's back rammed deeper. "Tell her to be quiet, or I shoot the dog."

"No, don't hurt her!" Lacey immediately stopped

twisting. "I'll go wherever you want to take me. Just don't hurt Promise."

"Don't get in that vehicle!" Wade rushed for her. If he could get the men off her and shield her from being shot, she could make a run for it.

A bullet sprayed the snow between them, halting Wade. The message was clear. There would be no running for either of them.

The men dragged Lacey to a black SUV in the shadows of the concession stand. The back door stood open and waiting. Promise refused to relinquish her hold on the man's pant leg. Lacey shouted, "Stay, Promise, stay with Wade," before being pushed inside the vehicle.

"Not to worry, Miss Phillips." The man stepped up behind Wade, the gun back in place. "You're both coming. Boss's orders."

Lacey's hands trembled on her lap where she'd sat for over an hour facing the rear window of the kidnappers' SUV. Promise nudged her, but she pushed the dog toward Wade to help him instead.

Except when Lacey glanced his way to her left, she noticed he was calm and collected and didn't need his service animal at the moment.

But then, why would he? His hypervigilance that plagued him during everyday peace times was warranted at the moment. It kept him in the right state of mind for the task at hand.

Operation Rescue.

He sat on one side of her while another man sat on her right. Two of the other gunmen sat across the seats facing them, weapons drawn. The man to her right had the dreaded capsule.

Wade folded his arms and bumped her wound. She

inhaled sharply, even though it was healing well. It did still pain her when touched, especially after these men had manhandled her.

"Sorry, I didn't mean to hurt you." Wade looked at the men across from him. "She was shot, but I guess you already know that."

No reply came, but Wade's attention never wavered from the kidnappers across from them. He also kept his hand on her arm with a gentle rub she could feel through the fabric of his army combat coat she still wore. His calmness made her think he'd been prepared for something of this nature. Knowing him, he'd probably even planned for it. He'd mentioned to her his duties included rescues, but did those ever include his own?

Wade continued to brush against her arm. Slowly, she relaxed and leaned a little closer in toward him, accepting the comfort he offered her. She trusted he would get them out of this before another hour of driving went by.

She could only wonder when Wade planned to make his move and what he would need her to do when he did.

"I'm surprised you haven't blindfolded us." Wade broke the void of the heavy silence. "That could only mean one thing."

No reply.

The car slowed and came to a stop. The driver's window lowered, and Lacey could hear the murmur of voices from the front. The driver was talking to someone outside, being very friendly.

Was it a police officer? Had they been pulled over? She hadn't seen any lights out the rear window, but someone was definitely out there. If so, this could be her only chance to be free.

"Don't even think about it." The guy to her left pressed his gun into the side of her rib cage.

The scream in her mouth escaped on a squeak. She glanced at Wade, expecting him to make his move now.

Instead, he winked.

He actually winked.

Lacey merely stared, wishing she could ask him how he could be so casual about this, especially when the SUV picked up speed again. That was when she saw out the rear window that they had just entered some sort of gated area. A small check-in station had been what the car had stopped off at.

Wade huffed. "You're military. I knew it."

Military? They were on a military base? Lacey studied the stolid faces across from her, so like Wade's full ops face on so many occasions. Men with a mission and a plan to carry it out.

But if she and Wade were in danger at the hands of the United States military, then that meant her brother had been, too.

Lacey's blood pressure skyrocketed in an instant. "Jeffrey was killed by his own men?" She shook her head, unable to fathom it. "He gave you his life. How could you?"

Wade's hand covered hers, but she didn't just feel his hand. She felt something hard in it.

Wade had managed to obtain some kind of weapon? But what?

The knife from his coat!

That was why he had been touching her arm. He was lifting it off her, out of the pocket in his uniform. He wasn't offering her comfort at all.

But he was trying to save her.

She would take it.

The car came to a stop in front of airplane hangar number 256, according to the numbers painted on the outside of the gray exterior walls. A plane flew overhead. By the sound, Wade determined it to be a tanker. The base was used for refueling, and now, apparently, kidnapping.

The man beside Lacey pulled her from the vehicle first, but Promise jumped out to take up her place beside Lacey immediately. Wade followed behind and silently promised there would be lots of treats for his dog later.

And there would be a later. Wade had every intention of putting an end to this charade tonight. For some reason, some superior up in ranks had deemed seizure as the best method of getting them here. They didn't know all it would have taken was an invite. Wade was ready to put this whole investigation to bed and would have RSVP'd promptly had he been given the opportunity. Of course, his gun would have been by his side in that scenario. Now he was walking in with nothing but the small knife he'd swiped from his combat jacket on Lacey. It was hardly enough against all the lead aimed at them, but it was something to help free her.

None of the men had any idea he'd taken it while he sat beside her in the SUV. At first he'd thought she knew he was up to something when she'd leaned into him, but at her tiny sigh, he'd seen she was only depending on him. That idea scared him more than this last mile they walked together.

The fool woman had no idea of the pain depending on him would bring to her life. There were whole days he lost during one of his bouts. What if she needed him and he let her down? What if he indirectly hurt her—the one person he would never want to cause pain? By allowing her into his life, it was bound to happen. She'd said she never wanted to get married because it was the people closest to her who could hurt her the most. And *she* was talking about people who didn't have PTSD.

No. There could never be anything between them. He wouldn't do that to her. He would get her out of here tonight and tell her to go live her life. He'd told her that before. He'd said it would be what Jeff would want for her. It was also what he wanted for her. A long, safe and happy life.

The first man in the line opened the side door and held it back for them all to pass through. They entered the open hangar, empty of any planes. Nothing but an eight-foot-long table and some chairs propped open. Two men stood behind the table as they were ushered in.

"Welcome," the eldest of the two spoke, his voice booming and influential. His tailor-made suit accentuated a strong physique. His bright white hair was the only thing that gave his age away. Wade estimated him to be pushing eighty, but he could pass for seventy. "Take her to the other room," the man instructed.

Wade took a step to grab Lacey's arm. "She stays with me."

"Nothing will happen to her. I just want to talk to you alone first." The man nodded to the guy who had pilfered Wade's gun back at the track. The guy gave Wade a smirk as he came up behind Lacey, his gun pointed at her.

Wade held tight to her, conflicted. "She takes the dog, then. I don't want her without protection."

The old man gave the nod.

Wade let go of her arm and pushed his dog forward. "Stay with Lacey, Promise. On her side. Don't leave her." Wade looked into Lacey's frightened eyes. "Keep that smart head of yours focused. And be ready to go."

"Always." Lacey stepped forward with Promise by her side.

"Agent—" the old man held out his hand to stop the guy herding Lacey "—you can leave the spike with me."

"Of course, sir. I forgot." He pulled the capsule from his suit's side pocket and handed it over.

They exited and the metal door banged closed. The sound jolted Wade's eyes shut before he straightened up to face the old man. "You said nothing would happen to her. I'm holding you to that."

Their shoes and Promise's paws tapped against the smooth concrete surface of a long darkened corridor. Lacey passed several doors. Was she being taken to the farthest room away from Wade in case she screamed? She didn't dare yell with so many guns on him. He would surely be shot trying to get to her. The horrid image pushed her forward, as well as the gun in her rib cage.

The last room went by. The only other door left was illuminated by an exit sign.

"You're not taking me out of here." Lacey twisted to go back, but the guy pushed the gun deep just as he had done in the car when she'd attempted to scream.

"You just lost your brother. Don't you want to know why?"

She hesitated at his words. Of course she wanted to know. But to leave the building to get the answers would be…impulsive. She would put herself right back in the line of fire *again*. She really would make herself a liability if she walked out that door. She needed to prove to Wade that he was wrong about her.

"No, I won't go." She tried to lock her legs. The gun jammed into her back. Lacey scrunched and cried in pain at the third time this guy had shoved her ribs tonight. She knew the drill. One push meant "I'm right behind you." Two meant "move it." This third push meant she'd been warned.

Lacey angled a last look at the end of the hall, knowing she didn't dare shout to Wade, but she might never see him again.

He'd said be ready to go, and that was all she could do. With each step closer to the door, she called on God for help. *Father God, You are my guide. You go before me to pave my way. I can walk in faith knowing that I don't walk alone, even when we don't know what's behind the next door. I can go where You lead me knowing You have plans for me. Greater plans than I or Wade could ever create. Plans to bring me hope and a future, to bring hope and a future to both of us, and never to harm us. Protect us both, Lord Jesus. And I pray Your plans bring Wade and I back together. I have his dog, and...and he has my heart.*

Lacey didn't know how it had happened. She'd always guarded her heart from anyone who might hurt her, and Wade was the one person who would hurt her. He admitted it daily.

But wasn't that keeping it real as she asked? Her whole reason of rejecting marriage was the veil that covered that truth. Wade never put on the blinders, and he never pretended.

"Let me go back." Lacey halted and whipped around. "I have to go back! I have to tell him I love him."

The next second, her head was smashed up against the concrete wall. Pain exploded through her whole body, and the air in her lungs whooshed out. She fell to her knees, grabbing her head.

"The only place you're going is out that door." The guy hit the bar on the door and dragged Lacey out through it. Promise barked just as a loud plane approached overhead. The door slammed shut behind them as Lacey was thrown to the asphalt.

She lifted her head to find a black Lexus Sport parked

by the door blocking her path. It took less than a second to remember this car from earlier in her travels.

She was blocked by Clay's car.

The guy behind her came around and opened the rear door. Clay sat quietly in the backseat.

Lacey's aching head rebelled against what this looked like.

Clay couldn't be the one who'd killed Wade's family. Or Jeffrey.

Wade loved this man like a father.

"Clay? What's going on? Why are you here?"

He frowned in the overhead light of the cabin. "You should have gone home, Lacey."

"No, Wade needs us. He needs you! He's inside and needs help!"

"That's all I ever meant to do. Help those kids."

"Well, come on. We need to rescue him right now. There are people who want to kill him in there."

A tear fell down the man's cheek, but he didn't budge one muscle. Lacey crawled as another plane grew closer and louder. "Come on, Clay!"

That was when she saw his hands and feet were tied.

"Get in the car, Lacey."

Lacey shrunk back, right into the knees of her guard. Only, it wasn't her guard, because her guard was in front of her, holding the car door.

Lacey turned to look up and found Clay's friend from earlier tonight, once again towering over her.

Senator Teigen said, "Clay was right. You should have gone home. Your brother didn't heed the warning, either."

Lacey heard Promise growl from deep in her throat.

"Take care of the dog," Teigen said to her guard. The gunman lifted his gun and took aim.

Lacey scrambled for Promise, but the senator pulled

her up by the waist. Her feet kicked out in front of her. "Run, Promise! Run away! Go!" Lacey yelled at the top of her lungs. The gunshot cut through the night, but only for a split second before the roar of the airplane's engine passing overhead swallowed the sound completely.

Promise ran away as she was told to do.

Lacey sagged back in relief. Wade would have his dog back.

Teigen dug his hands into the front pockets of Wade's combat coat. He removed some candy wrappers and papers and some red fabric. She remembered it was the sling she'd used on Christmas Eve, Clay's handkerchief. She hadn't even known it was in there. He shoved it all back in her pocket with lethal force. "Where is it? Where's the capsule?" He looked at her gunman. "I thought you messaged me that she found it."

Her gunman didn't look so frightening now. Instead, he seemed to cower. "Senator Teigen, I was bringing it to you, but Ackerman made me leave it in the hangar. I couldn't alert them to anything, so I had to follow orders."

"By ignoring mine?"

Lacey could only figure the guy in charge inside was this Ackerman they were talking about. Was this some sort of battle between Teigen and Ackerman? A race to see who would confiscate the capsule first?

Just great. Both her and Wade were stuck in the middle of two evil geniuses.

"But I got you the laptop you wanted, sir. It's hidden at the track," the gunman said. "Isn't that what you really wanted?"

"Yes. I'll let Ackerman have the capsule. I was supposed to release the film years ago and play the shocked friend, but this will work, too." Teigen looked into the car at Clay. "I tried to make sure you took the fall last time, even had your picture taken in the act of spying on Meredith for me—a lot of good it did when the film was taken by the kid. Your deaths won't be deemed an accident like the others had. This time they'll know it was you. When the film is developed and your car is found with you at the wheel and Miss Phillips in back, they'll think murder/suicide. It will look as if you couldn't go on living knowing what you did." Teigen reached into his pocket and withdrew a wet-looking rag, looking straight at Lacey. "And neither of you will be alive to tell otherwise."

Three thoughts ran through Lacey's mind as she saw the rag coming her way. The first thought was Teigen just might take the cup for most evil. The second thought was she had a cloth of her own in her pocket that might leave a trail. Her third thought as Teigen's rag hit her face and turned her mind fuzzy was if she would be fast enough to get hers out.

FIFTEEN

"Cut to the chase. Do you plan to kill us?" Wade stared down his nose at the old man.

The guy offered a chair, but Wade refused. "I can promise you, you have no reason to fear for your life. In fact, I'm the reason you're alive when your friend Jeff Phillips isn't."

"Then, tell your men to put their guns away," Wade said, calling his bluff.

"Okay. At ease, gentlemen."

Weapons clacked as all the men followed orders and put them away with no fuss.

The old man signaled Wade's closed fist. "Now you can put your knife away."

Wade wasn't surprised. These men were quite skilled. Slowly, he revealed the switchblade hidden in his palm, then placed it into his front jeans pocket. He scanned each face before landing his attention back on the old man. "Who are you?"

"My name is Michael Ackerman, but you would know me better as Gary Shelton."

Wade squinted. "Shelton. My mother's maiden name was Shelton. Gary Shelton was my grandfather."

"Yes. Your mother was my daughter."

Wade studied the man's face at the turn of these events. Twenty-eight years changed a man's appearance, and this guy didn't bring back any memories to vouch for him. Wade ground his teeth as he made his decision to run with it or not.

He chose not.

"My grandfather died of a heart attack when I was eight. Are you sure you weren't her espionage handler?"

"Interesting. Why do you think your mother was a spy?"

Wade swallowed hard. He drifted his attention to the capsule on the table. Ackerman stepped forward and opened the container to pour out its contents on the table.

A single roll of film.

Wade wasn't any closer to knowing its contents. It was old. There was a chance the film wouldn't even develop correctly. He might never know what information the capsule contained.

"You found this capsule as a child, correct?" Ackerman asked.

Wade wondered how he knew, but answered, "Affirmative. When I gave it to my mother, she said not to tell anyone about it. That tells me she knew what she was looking at. Add in her fake-identity documents I found when I was eighteen, and what am I supposed to think about her? Oh, and I should add, my father probably thought the same thing. He filed for divorce over it."

"There wasn't going to be a divorce. It had been called off."

"How do you know these things?"

"Because I made a promise to your father. I told him I would stay away from my daughter and never involve her in my life again if he called it off."

"So you *were* her handler."

"No. Your mother was not a spy, but I *was* CIA and her father. With that comes a life of assumed identities for her protection only. Not because she was involved in any counterintelligence. I believed I could have the family and the career without them overlapping. I was wrong. My wife was found by my Russian enemies and killed first. I still held on to the hope Meredith would be safe on her mountain, but when she was found and killed, I realized I had to end the identity of Gary Shelton forever. I couldn't let my grandchildren be used against me, too. Like I said, I'm the reason you're alive, but only because you thought I was dead. It was best this way."

Best this way?

Wade's words turned on him suddenly felt cheap. Was this how Roni felt when he said he couldn't come home?

Wade looked at the man who claimed to be his grandfather. "Twenty-eight years is a long time to play dead. Why not stay dead? Why bring me here to uncover everything you thought was best for us? Although, I really don't see how leaving two orphaned children alone is best or even safe."

"You were never alone. You had your uncle, and believe it or not, you still had me watching over you." Michael sent a wave toward the door Lacey and Promise had walked through. "That dog you have is one of the best. I made sure of it. She's trained to know a hundred commands more than the others in her group. You haven't even broken the surface with her yet. Wait until you see everything she can do, even sniff out danger and protect you from any harm."

"You arranged for me to have her?"

"I made sure you were on the top of the list." Michael took the chair he offered to Wade before. "I've read your reports. First, know that I'm very proud of you and all you've done for our country. But as proud as you've made me, there were times while I read through the files that I wept. I know the horrors you've lived through and saw, beginning with that car crash. It changed you. It took away your innocence. It created in you the inability to be still. When I learned you enlisted at eighteen, I wasn't surprised. Nor was I surprised every time you reenlisted. The army way of life allowed you to use your heedful state of mind and feel useful."

Wade nodded once. There was no reason to lie, especially if Wade wanted this guy to know he blamed him for his state of mind. "So my family and I were run off the road because someone found out we were your kin and they wanted to hurt you?"

Michael blinked. "When my Meredith called me to tell me someone was using the track for espionage, I knew she'd been located by my enemies. It had to be them using the track to spy on her to find something on me. She knew it, too. She was born into the CIA. She grew up with assumed identities and knowing all about dead drops and spikes and when to recognize danger. I told her to pack her family up and leave immediately for a safe house."

"We never made it off the street," Wade reminded him.

The cavernous hangar fell into heavy silence. After a heavy sigh, Ackerman asked, "How well do you know Lacey Phillips? Are you sure you can trust her? That she isn't out for her own gain?"

"She's innocent in all of this."

"She found the capsule. She knew where Meredith hid it when even I didn't."

"Lacey's brother figured it out, and was killed for it. She was only trying to finish what he started."

"And what was that?"

Wade bit down hard, but knew the truth when he saw it. "To bring some peace to my life."

After a few pensive seconds, Michael looked back at the table and picked up the film. "Then, we better figure out what's on this roll. Someone wanted it enough to kill for it. If you say we can trust her, I'll have her brought back in."

"I would trust her with my life."

"That's good enough for me." Michael gave the word to the men to retrieve Lacey and passed the film to one of his men with the directions to get it developed ASAP.

Wade breathed deep knowing Lacey would be back by his side in a few seconds.

Only a few seconds ticked into minutes. Doors could be heard slamming behind the metal door.

"I don't like this." Wade rushed for the entrance to the hall, but just as he made it to the door, it swung wide. A blanched serviceman stood on the other side.

"She's gone. Nobody's in there. I found these outside." He held up a red handkerchief and some candy wrappers. He also produced a business card. "The card belongs to Senator Teigen."

Wade reached for the fabric and card, his chest tightening at the sight of the cloth. "The handkerchief is my uncle's. It was in the pocket of my combat jacket she was wearing. The card must have been, too. The senator must have given it to her earlier tonight when they met. He was going to help her investigate her brother's death."

Wade turned to see Michael reading a handheld device. Was the man sending a text?

"What are you doing? We have to find her!" Wade rushed the table.

"That's what I'm doing, son."

"You can track her?"

"No." Michael turned the device. A blinking red dot moved along a map. It sure looked like a tracker to Wade. "But I can track Promise's collar. I put that collar on Promise before she was given to you. It's how I've been keeping up with you right along. Apparently, we've had a traitor in our midst who gave out this piece of intelligence for someone else to make use of."

"So that's how they've been showing up wherever we went. My dog was giving me away?"

"And now the collar's telling me the dog's moving along the perimeter of the base. Move out!"

The force moved into their positions like clockwork. They filed into the trucks and went in their own strategized directions. Wade sat in the same rear seat of the SUV he came in on, now working with the men he knew were cut from the same cloth as him.

Everyone but that traitor who had held him up...and seemed to enjoy it just a little too much. Wade had known that guy was sick. And now he had Lacey.

The trucks sped along the base roads, then over snow, until Michael yelled, "There she is!"

Wade crouched by the door to see Lacey. He scanned the area, but the only one in sight was Promise running at full tilt, alone. Wade banged his fist on the window.

Lacey was gone.

SIXTEEN

Promise whined beside Wade from the backseat of the SUV. Michael Ackerman and his operatives were inside the hangar discussing their next move while they waited for the film to be developed.

Wade anxiously fiddled with Clay's red handkerchief while thoughts of Lacey made him want to run with no destination in mind.

Promise nosed his hand to get his attention, causing Wade to drop the cloth to the floor. His fists clenched to keep from touching her. Wade couldn't give her a second of his focus. He was wound so tight he thought he might shatter into a million pieces.

This wasn't the first time he'd felt like this. The first time had been when he was eight years old and he was told his parents and baby brother, Luke, were gone forever. Numerous other times during his life he'd fought against this same feeling, always believing if he refocused on the plan, he could overcome it.

But what was *it* that he needed to overcome?

Promise licked his hand, growing more frantic. She barked up at him with one loud "Woof!" and pawed his arm.

Wade looked down to see his hands and arms shaking. No amount of refocusing would stop them. He knew it as surely as the morning sun could be seen rising over the mountains. How many times had he tried to stop the reaction? How many times had he lost?

Promise head butted him.

"Stop it!" Wade yelled in her face. "Can't you see I'm trying to focus? Can't you see I'm in more pain than I've ever been? I can't lose her, Promise. I just can't. I can't lose another person I love."

Promise pushed her head up, nose in the air, unfazed by his outburst. But her eyes drooped with glistening understanding and sensitivity...and love.

Wade reached for her and grabbed the sides of her furry head. He latched on and let her love bring him back down from his fear.

Fear. That was the *it* he'd tried so hard to overcome. It had surrounded his life for so long he barely remembered a time it didn't consume him. It left him with a wound that would never heal. Sure, he could refocus on the plan to bring some control back over his life. He could convince himself that he was winning and even healed, but the healing was superficial and equivalent to a scab covering everything up. A scab waiting to be torn off to start the whole process over again.

And over again.

And over again.

And over again... Unless he opened his mouth and faced it.

Words were powerful, as Jeff had said. But could Wade actually talk? What if admitting to his fear had the power to break him even more?

"But what if it doesn't?" Wade spoke into the empty car.

No. Not empty. His battle buddy was here with him,

and she was ready to wage war against his fear. He could see it in her brown, liquid eyes. She was waiting for him to tell her all his darkest secrets. It was what she'd been trained for. Nothing he said to her would hurt her. She was taught to take it all and hold no judgments in return. And whatever he said, she would take it to her grave.

She'd promised.

Wade let out a sigh and as he refilled his lungs, he blurted the words, "I am so scared. I am so scared." The words just kept coming, tumbling over each other until tears blurred his vision and Promise licked them from his face. Wade burrowed his face into the fur of her neck and cried for all the years he wouldn't let himself. Not when he was eight. Not when he was eighteen. Not when he'd lost his first comrade in battle. Not when he'd lost his twenty-first.

The tears quieted down, but his breath still came in short sporadic inhales. Wade knew what he had to do before he could take one step more.

"I'm ready for You, Jesus. I'm done charting my own course to an unknown destination. All I ever do is go in circles, reliving the horrors over and over again. From now on, I will follow the plan You have for my life. I surrender it all to You. Lacey—" Wade's voice cracked at her name on his lips. "Lacey thinks You will lead me. That I'm worth something to You. I want to believe this. I want to belong to You. And I want to believe You will lead me to her before it's too late. Please, Lord, lead me."

Promise whined in his ear and shuffled her body backward. She let out a "Woof!" and wagged her tail from her spot.

Just then a tap came on the window. It was the suit who was supposedly his grandfather. "We've got a face and a name, and we're tracing his car. But you're not going to like it. It might be best if you stay here."

Wade lowered the window. "Who is it?"

Michael hesitated, but turned his handheld device around to show a picture of a younger version of Clay.

"You think my uncle took her? That doesn't make any sense. He would never do anything like that."

As he denied the accusation, he looked down at the red cloth spilling over his boot like blood. Had this been a message from Lacey? Had she dropped it so he would know his uncle was behind it all? The real traitor in all of this?

The biggest sucker punch ever nearly bowled Wade over. He snatched up the cloth and papers she'd left behind and stuffed them in his pocket.

"I'm going with you," Wade announced.

"You're too close to this. It might be best—"

"I'm tired of doing what's best. Get in."

Michael opened the door. "We're not taking the cars. It'll be faster to chopper out."

"Perfect. Now you're speaking *my* language." Wade jumped from the SUV.

So this was what it was like to follow God's plan. Wade's feet had never felt so sure.

Intense cold jolted Lacey from her sleep. She flashed her eyes wide, inhaling deep and choked. Water. She was lying in frigid water in the backseat of a car. She tried to push up, but her arms refused to budge from their place behind her. Her hands were bound. Pulling harder only made her roll her body off the seat. She yelped when she hit the floor and sank deep into icy liquid. The shock at the temperature had her body writhing in panic and sputtering.

She pushed back and got her first view of the side window covered in murky water.

She was in a car sinking to the bottom of a lake!

"Help!" she screamed. "Help me!"

Adrenaline came through her confusion. Her bound hands against the floor and her stomach muscles joined in to push her body up to a sitting position. Over the top of the seat, she could see someone sat at the wheel.

A man. He was slumped over, unconscious.

Lacey shivered in the water filling the car. How long before it reached the ceiling?

She used her palms again to lift her body up out of the water and to her back on the seat. The sunroof above showed light shining through.

She wasn't fully submerged…yet.

The sunroof was her ticket out of here, though. But how with her hands tied?

"Hey!" she yelled to the guy. She pushed harder. Grinding her teeth, she used her feet to sit up on the seat—and get her first glimpse of the driver.

Clay.

The scene at the base flooded back. Teigen had said he'd planned that Clay take the fall for this. Teigen must have knocked Clay out and put him behind the wheel before pushing the car in…a murder/suicide, just as he'd said.

But she wasn't dead yet!

Lacey frantically looked to see if Clay was.

His hands weren't bound like hers. Could he be revived?

With Clay awake, he might be able to get them both out of here. Or at least he could save himself. Wade needed him.

Without this man in his life, Wade would very likely

close up forever. Lacey had to do everything in her power to make sure that didn't happen.

She pushed herself to kneel and lean forward over the front seat on her stomach. Immediately, the car jerked and more water gushed in. Lacey picked up her speed, jabbing her shoulder into Clay's slumped back. "Clay! Wake up! You've got to get out of here. We're going to drown. Clay!"

His head moved to the other side, but he gave no sign of hearing.

"Clay! You've got to help Wade! Can you hear me? Wade needs you!"

"Wade?" Clay shot up straight, but quickly let out a loud groan. He reached for his head where blood dripped. Water sloshed around his waist, jolting him. "Huh? Wh—" He looked around. "What's going on?"

Panic set in as the man fumbled with the understanding of his surroundings.

"Clay, listen to me." Lacey tried to bring his focus to her. Uncertainty crossed his face. He couldn't place her in his confused state.

"It's me, Lacey, Wade's friend. You need to get out of this car. It's sinking to the bottom of a lake. You've got to break the window above and swim out as fast as you can. Get help. I can't do anything with my hands tied."

The blank look on his face remained. Had he heard anything she said? "I did this. I helped Chuck."

"You helped him put the car in the lake?"

"It was all a lie. He used me." Clay's vacant look snapped away. "He made me think I was serving my country by spying on Meredith for him. He learned who Meredith's father was and said the government was looking for a link to him. I wasn't joking when I said Gary Shelton was mafia. Chuck told me he was Russian mafia.

We used the track to get and pass information to each other, but Chuck was also using it to pass information to someone else. It was why he pushed for the track's opening at the state level. It had nothing to do with jobs. He wanted to take down Meredith and Gary. I believed him when he said they worked for the Russians. Times were heated then. I couldn't let her hurt our country and my family. But it was all a lie. Chuck was the one making the deals with the Russians."

Lacey felt her mouth drop. "Are you saying you knew the Spencers would be pushed over the ledge?"

"No! I didn't! That was an accident. The police said so."

"No, Clay, it was murder."

"No. No." He shook his head, but soon crumpled, unable to deny it any longer.

"And we're about to be murdered, too, by the same killer. Please get out of here. Get through the window before we sink. Wade needs you."

"He needs *you*. You love him. I know you do. I didn't believe you for a second when you said you didn't."

"Yes, I do. I do love him, but you're his family. He can't lose you. He's lost too many already. Please, just do as I ask."

"Here, let me untie you." Clay knelt to reach her. The car tilted back and more water gushed in. The current pushed Lacey back at full force, straight to the back of the hatchback.

"No time! Go!" She tried to speak through the water hitting her face and holding her down.

"I can't leave you!"

"Go!"

The command pushed Clay into motion. He flipped

to his back and lifted his leg to kick up and out the sun-roof. But nothing happened.

He kicked again and again. The car creaked and groaned and slipped deeper down. A current poured in; Clay finally pushed through the glass.

Relief for Wade rushed in, even as gushing water pushed Lacey down, keeping her there. There was no three-push warning this time. This was it, and in this final moment it wasn't about pushing back or going where God led. It was about trusting Him and letting go.

SEVENTEEN

"The ice on the pond isn't solid enough to land on!" The pilot's voice came through the headsets of the three passengers on board the helicopter. Clay's car had been traced to this mountain location where he used to live in the old caretaker's cabin. They'd passed over the pond and were circling back around to look for an open space in the thick growth of trees. No open, flat land could be seen to bring the helicopter down on.

"How about the road?" Wade suggested as he scanned the area below. He saw an open space on the road, but it was a distance away. It would require a half-mile run, time they didn't have.

Michael swung around from his passenger seat. "How do you feel about rappelling down?"

"Could be dangerous on my own without a rappel guide."

"Is that a yes?"

Wade thought of Lacey, but not just the danger she was in. He thought of her motto in life. Go unless God told her no. "Affirmative."

"We'll get the chopper down below seventy-five feet. Gear up. Agent Samson, help Wade as best you can. And, Wade, go slow."

With the help of the agent, Wade prepped a deployment bag that would be tossed out before he began the descent. He removed his headset to fit the helmet to his head. All audio communication would now cease with the men in the chopper. A pair of all-leather gloves came next. The double-leather palms and fingers would provide protection from the intense heat created by his hands on the slide down the rope. He grabbed the safety belt with a harness and tether. In a moment the nylon rope would be his only lifeline. Before fitting them on, he emptied his pockets for a snug fit. The red cloth and papers fell to his seat.

Again the cloth turned his stomach.

He would be rappelling down to save Lacey from his uncle, the one person Wade thought would never hurt him. Lacey was right. It was the people closest to us who could hurt us the most. But Wade would make sure Clay paid for all his crimes and for taking away the people Wade loved most…including Clay. The pain ripped him apart, but he gritted his teeth and prepared for his jump.

Geared up, Wade gave a thumbs-up to the pilot. He was ready.

The pilot swooped the helicopter back out over the pond. Wade leaned in to the turn and looked down at the cloth and papers again. The business card with Senator Charles Teigen's name printed across the middle faced up. Wade read the line below his name and froze.

A slogan for the senator's latest campaign screamed at Wade from the card.

"Words are Powerful: Vote for Literacy."

Those powerful words blared louder in Wade's head than the rotating blades of the helicopter.

Teigen was the direction Jeff was sending him. Teigen was why Jeff had been killed.

Jeff had gone after a dirty senator, the man responsible for killing Wade's family. The true spy and traitor.

Wade called to his grandfather, holding the card up, but no one could hear him. Wade leaned in and shoved the card in Michael's face. His grandfather caught on quick and did a search for Teigen on his phone. Photographs came up, new ones then old. Michael showed an image that popped up.

An old campaign photo of a familiar-looking man from Wade's nightmares lit the screen. The man from the grandstand, and a much younger Senator Teigen.

There was no doubting it now.

All these years it had been him under the grandstand, a friend of Clay's. And now he had Lacey at the cabin.

Suddenly, Agent Samson hit Wade's back. He pointed out the opened door for Wade to look. Wade saw nothing but an expanse of the partially frozen pond.

The helicopter raced west, over freezing water. It shied north and approached the cabin.

That was when Wade saw the front end of a black car protruding out of the pond, contrasted against the silvery ice.

Wade shouted at the top of his lungs, "Go!" He knew no one heard anything above the noise of the whomping blades, but Lacey was in that car. He just knew it.

Wade grabbed the rope and nearly jumped out without going through the protocol of safety. The agent warned him by mouthing, "Slow down!"

But Lacey was going under!

Wade gave a stiff nod and performed the final check of the hookup, rappel seat, rappel ring. He pulled on the rope to double-check the anchor-point connection. A few hundred feet took them closer to the sinking car. Wade's heart plummeted right along with it as he went through the steps that slowed him down.

Wade threw out the rope, but still there were more steps. Wade never wanted to rush through them more than in this moment. Always he'd been a stickler to the rules of safety. *Slow and steady wins the race. Slow is smooth and smooth is fast.*

Lacey's motto never looked so good.

He sent the deployment bag out and away from the helicopter. He made sure the rope didn't fall between the side of the chopper and the skid legs used for when the chopper lands. Wade looked down to prove the rope was indeed touching a frozen piece of ice near the car and also free of tangles and knots. He then took his place in the door.

Ordinarily this was where things got intense, but the real intensity was knowing Lacey was in that car sinking into freezing water below, and he might never see her alive again.

Wade braced himself for the jump. On a one-hundred-eighty-degree pivot, he stood out on the skid, facing the inside of the helicopter. His feet were shoulder-width apart, his knees locked, the balls of his feet on the skid and his body bent at the waist toward the helicopter. He placed his brake hand on the small of his back and told Promise to stay. The dog looked as if she was smiling.

He gave the nod and the signal to go never felt so good.

Wade flexed his knees and vigorously pushed away from the skid gear. He let the rope pass through his brake hand to his guide hand. The descent sped by at eight feet a second, with no jerky stops. The rope zipped through his hands smooth and clean.

Wade shot a look at the car, now barely above the surface, speeding his way.

When his feet touched, he quickly cleared the rappel rope through the rappel ring to free the rope. Samson signaled above that he was off rappel, and he dropped the rope away from the helicopter.

Wade turned around and took off in a run on cracking ice. He pushed faster to get to the car; now only the front bumper protruded.

A loud burst from below his feet knocked him to his knees. The seeping, freezing water barely fazed him as he elbowed the rest of the way to the car and to Lacey.

The sheet of ice beneath him pushed up. At the same time the car slipped below the surface in a blink of an eye.

"Lacey!" Wade called and reached for a connected piece of ice. He slid over to it just as a hand reached out from the water.

Lacey!

Wade reached the edge and grabbed hold of the hand splashing the icy water.

It was not a female's.

Wade shimmied over to his left and grabbed the forearm of the man to get a better grip. The man came up sputtering and heaving for air. It was Clay.

"Where's Lacey?"

Clay still heaved on his belly, but gestured with weak hands that she was down below. "Backseat. Tied up. She made me leave her. I'm so sorry!" Clay could be heard yelling, but Wade was already entering the water.

The water sliced right through him like a million sharp knives. He ignored the pain and moved his arms to pull his whole body down. The car was just within reach, still floating with its back end deeper. Wade debated which side he should try for. Would the door be unlocked?

With time so critical, he could only pray. *Lord, guide me and I will steer Your way.*

Wade went left.

The front seats were empty as expected, and Wade reached for the handle of the back door. He fumbled when he saw Lacey floating in the backseat, unmoving.

He was too late, the thought came, but he still pulled the door wide and swam in to pull her into his arms and out of the car.

With her cradled in his arms, her head floating back to expose her slender neck, Wade kicked up with all his strength to the surface.

Ice blocked his path above, but a quick maneuver opened his passage clearly enough for him to push through with Lacey headfirst. Wade could only hope it would be in time.

Her body was quickly removed from Wade's arms. He grabbed hold of the ice and used the edge as leverage to free himself from the water. It cracked and broke off beneath him. He reached for a large broken-off piece to climb up on and get out of the freezing water.

Clay held Lacey, crawling with her to shore. Wade's grandfather and Samson could be seen running down the road from where they'd landed the chopper, a bag and blanket in hand. Would they reach Lacey to help her in time?

Wade pushed his piece of ice closer to the large one Lacey was on. The ice popped and cracked when he got on. "I can't get to her!" he yelled to Samson, who ran up to the shore. "The ice is breaking!"

"Come in a different way! I can get her from my side!" Samson crawled his way out onto the ice toward Lacey, taking her from Clay, who couldn't pull her anymore. He needed medical attention, as well. His body seemed to be fading fast from his cold plunge.

Wade moved as close to Lacey as he could without

causing her to cave back into the ice-cold water. Samson moved her onto a wool blanket and tried to revive her, but Wade was too far to touch and too far to help.

His gut twisted at the sight of her unconscious face. Lips of purple surrounded by stark white undid him. "Come on, Lacey!" he yelled to her. "You've got to wake up. Please, Lacey. Don't give up. Come back to me!"

Wade couldn't take his eyes off her for one second. Not even to hear the uncommon bark of his dog. Promise waited for him to look her way and to assure her he was all right. Her barks picked up to a crescendo.

"Wade, you're hyperventilating," Samson said from across Lacey. "Take slow, deep breaths through pursed lips, or you're going to go into cold shock. Get yourself to shore quickly."

Wade followed the directions for the breathing, but he couldn't leave Lacey. He spared a glance at his barking dog, but Promise wasn't looking at him. She was facing the woods. Her barks continued, but the sound of Lacey coughing stole his attention.

Water spurted out of her mouth and Samson turned her on her side. More ingested water released from her lungs and her eyelids parted but quickly shut again. Samson turned her onto her back.

"She's breathing. But I need to get her off the ice and warmed. Wade, we have to get her to shore without falling in. I'm going to try to pull her along."

Wade couldn't feel his hands against the ice anymore, but he managed to move toward shore little by little. Ice cracked beneath him. He dared not move closer to Lacey in case it broke through. But this meant he couldn't help Samson pull Lacey in. His weight wouldn't allow it.

Promise barked and padded onto the ice in a run toward him. She reached him, but her face seemed a little blurry, and her barks seemed to be growing softer. She licked him, but even that he couldn't feel. He figured he must be frozen to the point that his senses were shutting down. He reached for Promise's furry neck and saw how his fingers barely bent. They didn't look real hanging there in front of his face.

But they also weren't shaking.

"See, P-Promise, I'm okay, girl. But Lacey needs you. H-h-help L-L-Lacey."

The dog bumped her head to his.

"Help L-L-Lacey."

Promise ran over to Lacey as she was told to do.

Wade hoped the ice would hold his dog, especially when she started pulling on the blanket with her teeth. Each pull, Wade held his breath then released it when they moved a little closer to shore.

"Keep going!" Wade yelled. At least he thought he yelled. A slow realization came to his mind that he didn't actually say anything. Samson's words flashed in his mind. He'd warned Wade about cold shock.

Wade's eyelids grew heavy, but he shook his head to keep them open. He would be no use to Lacey if he went into shock, too. He looked to shore and saw her being picked up and transferred to the ground. Wade saw Clay draped in a blanket with Michael standing by him, a hand on his shoulder. A movement in the trees behind them caught his eye.

Someone was watching from behind a tree.

Wade looked to the face of the man.

Chuck Teigen.

Air whooshed from Wade's lungs. He tried to push up off the ice, but his appendages had shut down. This was the man who'd put the deaths of Wade's family into action when Wade had opened his mouth and told.

Wade opened his mouth again to alert his grandfather to the danger in their presence, to finally speak the truth and end the hold Teigen had had on his life for so long. Wade opened his mouth to talk, but no matter how much he tried, no words would come out.

Not even when the man stepped out of the trees and lifted a gun, aimed straight for Lacey.

Wade slapped the ice, hoping to get someone's attention. Promise ran back out to him, pacing around him. Wade grabbed the fur at her neck. He turned her to face the trees. "At-tack." Wade was unsure if Promise even knew that command.

But the smart dog shot off. Her strong muscular body took her back to shore; her legs lifted her high off the ground in her swift sprint. She zeroed in on Teigen's back, coming up behind him without his knowledge. With stealth and precision she took her last leap and soared through the air just as the gun exploded.

EIGHTEEN

The beeps of the heart monitor assured Wade that Lacey was still with him. Thanks to Promise, Teigen's gun had missed its mark, but that didn't change the doctors' diagnosis of her.

Too long under freezing water, they said. Low cardiac output in the rewarming phase after rescue. Extended time of hypoxia. All things Wade had heard spoken by medical personnel over the course of twenty-four hours. But the worst thing uttered: possible low functioning capabilities when she awakened, *if* she woke up at all.

Wade dropped his forehead to her weak, lifeless hand, so unlike her strong hands that controlled two thousand pounds of metal and six hundred horses under the hood.

But would she again?

If what the doctors said about her being low functioning did occur, would Lacey ever drive any car again?

"I'll take you anywhere you want to go," Wade said aloud, but he knew it could be so much worse than that. It could mean an inability to speak. It could mean she would be forever wheelchair bound. It could mean a totally different Lacey.

"Hey," a whisper came from the door behind him.

Wade looked up to see his sister coming in with two

cups of coffee. She stopped at the foot of the bed. "No change," he told her before she asked for the tenth time that day.

Roni brought the cup to him, but he wasn't ready to let go of Lacey's hand. She put it on the side table with the other coffee she'd brought in that morning. His breakfast also sat there uneaten.

"You were admitted, too, Wade. You need sustenance to get well. If you won't do it for yourself, then do it for Lacey. She's going to need you to be strong."

Wade swallowed hard. "You're right. She's going to need someone who's strong…and whole. Someone who's capable of not losing it when she needs him most. Someone who's not me."

Roni was quiet for a few minutes. Then she slumped down in the corner chair. "I did this."

Wade questioned her with a silent look.

"I'm sorry, Wade. I haven't been fair to you. I've guilted you every chance I could get to make you come home, throwing out that you needed to heal, as if there was something wrong and sick in you."

"There is."

"No, there isn't. Yes, you're injured. You've had to face a lot of heavy, scary stuff that left a mark on you no different than the marks on my neck and arm. You've never made me feel inadequate because of my wound, but I haven't done the same for you. I've reminded you constantly that it exists, and that's made you think something is wrong with you. But Lacey…" Roni drifted her attention to the bed. "She's been able to do what I never could."

Wade studied Lacey's soft, relaxed face. Her coloring had returned, but the smudges beneath her eyes still remained. "What's that?"

"Love you the way you are. She's not blind. She knows you hurt. She knows you might never love her back."

"I love her back," Wade said. "I love her so much it scares me. What if..."

"What *if* you live to be a hundred with her by your side? What *if* she wants to support you on your good days and your bad days?"

"That's the problem. You heard the doctor. Lacey hasn't woken up yet, and they're already prepared for the worst. What if I can't be there for her because of my bad days? That's the what-if I'm talking about."

Promise lifted her head from her slumber at his feet. She sniffed the air and resettled herself when she saw she wasn't needed to calm him. But that could change at any moment.

"Lacey deserves someone who can support her all the time, someone who can guide her and be her spotter for the dangers that come her way. And trust me, there're plenty of them. I've never seen a person get herself in so many mishaps." Wade felt his lips tug into a smile.

"Which you were there for, right down to dropping out of a helicopter and diving into freezing-cold water to get to her in time."

Wade knew what his sister was trying to do. "Because I was having a good day. But what if—"

"Oh, stop with the what-ifs. Nobody can be on 24/7. And if Lacey only loves you when you're perfect, then she really doesn't love you at all. She's seen you at your worst and she's seen you at your best, and her love stays the same. The question is, will you love her at her worst?"

Lacey heard the question clear as day. No longer were words muddied in her brain. Nothing was distorted or confusing, as they were when she was pulled from the water. She held her breath now and waited to hear Wade's answer before opening her eyes.

"No." His reply came sharp and resonated in the room.

Tears instantly filled behind Lacey's closed eyelids. The stab of pain was worse than she thought possible. Wade would never love her.

"I see," Roni said quietly, as though she could read Lacey's heartbreaking thoughts.

"No, you don't, Roni. You don't understand. I don't consider anything to be Lacey at her worst. Even her impulsiveness is who she is, and I would never want to change that in her. I love everything about her, and if she wakes up a different person, I will love that Lacey, too. But it will not be me loving her at her worst. It will be me loving her as the person she is."

After a few quiet seconds, Roni said, "I stand corrected. What say you, Lacey?"

Wade turned away from his sister. Lacey could barely see him through the blur of tears spilling down the sides of her face, pooling into her pillow. He jumped to his feet, still holding her hand, closing in on her. His free hand cupped the side of her face.

"Lacey, you're awake. Does anything hurt? Roni, get the doctor!"

Roni ran from the room as Lacey tried to push up.

"Wait, don't move. How does your head feel?"

"Foggy but okay."

He looked to her legs and she moved them under the blankets.

"Legs, check," he said. "And arms? How are your arms?"

Lacey lifted her arms and reached for him. At his sigh, he leaned in so she could wrap them around his neck and assure him she really was all right. He breathed deep against her ear, praying thanks to God for her healing.

Lacey pulled back, needing to see his face to be sure. "Wade, does this mean you've accepted God's love?"

"And anything else He wants to give me."

More tears sprang to her eyes. Could she hope that he would accept love from others, too? "How about Promise's love?"

Promise appeared beside Wade with her two front paws on the edge of the bed. Her tongue hung out in excitement.

"Down, Promise," Wade commanded. "Sorry, she just wants to make sure she did her job. You'll get your treat later, girl."

"She saved me?"

"Yeah, took Teigen right down. There's no denying it, she loves you."

"And you."

Wade smiled. "And me."

More hope blossomed in Lacey. Could he accept her love, too? There was only way to find out. "I lo—"

Voices from the door interrupted her. People elbowed each other to get in first, only stepping aside for the doctor.

"Well, well, you gave this group a big scare, young lady. I'm Dr. Monroe and I'm glad to see you awake and looking so much better than you did when you were flown in." The doctor studied her vitals as Lacey tried to make sense of what he was saying.

"Flown?"

"The helicopter on-site made all the difference for you. It's not too often an accident victim has a chopper ready and waiting to whisk them off to the hospital."

Lacey looked at Wade behind the doctor, then to the rest of the people at the door. "Mama, Daddy, what are you doing here?"

Her parents stepped up to her bedside, opposite the doctor. "We came right away, and thanks to Wade's grandfather, we had our own private plane waiting for us at the airport."

"What grandfather?" Lacey asked. There was so much she was missing.

A man in the doorway said, "That would be me. I'm Michael Ackerman, Wade and Veronica's grandfather."

"Ackerman?" Lacey pushed up on her elbows and heard the heart monitor pick up beeps.

Michael raised a hand. "I apologize for abducting you. When your brother started asking questions about my daughter's accident, he became a person of interest. Unfortunately, that carried over to you when you picked up the baton after his death. I wish I could have met him. He was a hero."

"Jeffrey was a hero?"

Wade stepped back to her side and cupped her hand. "A true hero. Senator Teigen's latest campaign slogan was Words are Powerful. That's what Jeff was trying to lead us to. Thanks to him, we now know it was Teigen who made deals with the Russians. Jeff wasn't writing a book after all. It was code to where all his research was planted. You should see all the pictures he had on Teigen, going back forty years. Those pictures are worth thousands of words and will put him away for life."

"Jeffrey died a hero," Lacey said with a slow smile. Somehow the words came easier knowing this. "And your mom was innocent. You must be so relieved."

"Not as relieved as I am to see you awake."

Michael Ackerman, aka Wade's grandfather, went on to explain the rest of the story, from the car crash to when Lacey found the capsule that no one had been able to locate. And how even that had been part of Teigen's plan to cover his involvement in the spying. He'd had photos of Clay taken and was supposed to pick the capsule up to use the film as blackmail. But Wade had found it first and alerted his mother to what was happening at her track. Unfortunately, it had been too late.

Lacey lifted her chin to Ackerman when he'd finished. "But what about Wade and Roni? How could you leave them when they needed their family?"

"Trust me, it was the hardest thing I've ever done, but it was for their safety that I broke off all connections to them. I'd already lost my wife and daughter. I took peace knowing that Wade and Veronica lived on, even if I had to watch them from afar. My death put an end to anyone trying to hurt me by hurting them."

Lacey looked back at Wade, but he no longer stood behind the doctor. She searched the room and found him against the wall, edging closer to the door. "Where do you think you're going?" Didn't he know she wanted him by her side?

"You've heard it all, and you have your family with you now," he said as though that was supposed to mean something to her. "We'll be out in the hall. Come, Promise. Come on, everyone."

"But I need you here. Beside me."

Wade looked from Lacey to her parents. Her father tugged on his wife's arm to pull her back to give Wade the place closest to Lacey. The invitation was loud and clear. The place by Lacey's side belonged to Wade. Lacey didn't know what she would do if he rejected it. She decided she wouldn't give him the chance.

"I love you, Wade." The words came out with a force this time—and a dare to turn her love away.

Wade stepped up to the bottom of the bed, but still

not by her side. His blues flashed at her declaration. His dimple turned rigid.

"Being loved upsets you?"

"Think about what you're saying, Lacey. A life with someone who isn't whole is bound to hurt you. I would rather die than harm one hair on your head."

"Even if I have perpetual helmet hair?"

"I'm being serious."

"So am I. I want to make sure you know that I'm not one of those girls who cares about her hair being out of place."

"I don't care about your hair! I care about your heart and breaking it."

Lacey put her hand on her heart. "Now I love you even more. I'll never find another guy who will love me despite my messy hair."

His lips pressed into an angry line. "Your hair is hardly equal to what my brokenness will do to you. Can't you see that?"

Lacey looked at her mother and understood her wise words to her at the shop even more now. Lacey would hug her later for it.

She looked back at Wade and lifted her chin. "You can push me away all you want, but nothing will change the way I feel about you. I will always love you, and if you walk out that door, I will still love you. And not for anything you think you can offer me. Sure, I can list all the wonderful qualities that make loving you easier, but it's the man beneath it all who has my heart, and you will have it forever. Good days, bad days and every day in between are just more days for me to show it with my truth and actions. Can't you see *that*?"

Wade stepped around the bed, but the look on his face didn't look anything but livid. "You're asking me to be okay with hurting you because you love me. Do you know how ridiculous and selfish on my part that sounds? What kind of man would I be if I accepted those terms?"

"An honest one."

He stilled beside her, studying her face.

"How many people promise to love and cherish someone only to hurt them because they denied a weakness in their life? It's why I never wanted to get married. I didn't trust someone who pledged their undying love when things were going well. Can they still say they will feel the same when things aren't? I can. Our honesty now will only make us stronger together later. With everything in the light, there can be no hidden surprises."

"It's going to be hard, Lacey," Wade said in a rush on a raspy whisper.

"I drive race cars, Wade. Do I look like some wimpy girl?"

"I want marriage, Lacey. Nothing else."

"Is that a proposal?"

Wade pulled back. The shocked look on his face at the turn this conversation just took had him switching gears. He looked around the room at their family's expectant eyes. "Wait. I can't do this."

Everyone started to shuffle out of the room to give them privacy.

"Stay where you are." Wade stopped them in their tracks. "I want everyone I love here."

Instead, it was Wade who left the room, leaving an awkward silence and flittering glances that didn't reach Lacey's eyes.

Wade suddenly reappeared in the doorway, Clay's forearm held in his grasp.

Clay kept his eyes downcast from everyone in the

room. One look and Lacey knew he felt responsible for all that happened.

"Clay," she said, knowing Wade needed this man in his life. "You don't need to take this on as your fault. You trusted an old friend who used you."

Clay's shoulders curved in, his eyes avoided hers. So different he was from the night she met him on Christmas Eve. "I shouldn't have been in denial for so long. Deep down, I knew the truth of the accident. No. The murder. I was living a lie."

"It allowed you to feel safe, Clay. Sometimes the parties and gates fill a role for a time, but sooner or later, they have to come down and the truth has to be dealt with. It's the only way we can heal. I think the blinders are off for everyone now. Wouldn't you agree?"

Clay nodded because his emotions wouldn't let him speak.

"So let the healing begin." She looked at Wade. "For everyone."

Wade's blue eyes pierced her to the point she lost her breath. He moved back to her side, and his hand found her cheek. Tears filled his eyes, making them glassy and shimmering. "I don't deserve you."

"That's a Jesus kind of love. Because of Jesus, we don't get what we deserve. We get loved instead. Will you let me love you?"

Clay cleared his throat. "If you'll allow me to speak. Just some fatherly advice, Wade. This is a very special lady. If I were you, I wouldn't let her go."

Wade smiled down at her. "All she knows how to do is go. It's her motto for everything."

"Then, perhaps you might want to jump in and go with her." The room of people giggled at Clay's remark.

Promise jumped up on the bed to lick Lacey's face.

Wade pulled Promise back, concern on his expression. "Promise, down. Lacey's injured."

"Then, I couldn't think of a better dog to help me heal. She's the most gentle and attentive dog ever. Will you share her with me?"

Lacey patted the side of the bed for Wade to sit, but Promise claimed the spot before he could.

"I see how this is going to go."

Lacey laughed even though Wade wasn't. "So serious you always are." She mocked him to get a smile, but it didn't work. Then Promise pushed her head into his hand, and Lacey could see a smile about to crack. This dog was good medicine.

"Move it, Promise. It's my turn to smother her with kisses." Wade slid his hand to the back of her head and leaned down.

Lacey locked her eyes on his lips, ready to claim hers. She waited for the confetti that was sure to shoot off around her at any second, more mind-blowing than any winner's circle she would ever be in. She rushed up to meet him.

Wade pulled back. "Not so fast, my little need-for-speed. We're doing this my way."

Lacey rolled her eyes. "Oh, brother. You all might as well come back tomorrow. This could take a while."

Wade laughed, his deep rich baritone she rarely heard, and honestly, wasn't in any rush to hear go away.

"Lacey Phillips, I think you're crazy."

"Well, thanks, I love you, too."

"That's why I think you're crazy. How you could ever love me will forever boggle my mind. You humble me and honor me and stupefy me all at the same time. But if you will marry me, I promise I will spend the rest of my life cherishing you and loving you with everything I have in me, and then some. I won't lie and say the road ahead of us won't be bumpy, it will be, but with us going together, and God and honesty as our guides, it will be an incredible race."

Lacey smiled. "I see where you're going with this," she said with a slow nod. "I might even let you drive."

"First you have to say yes, then our first trip will be to the church. Right away. Like this weekend."

"So fast? That's so unlike you, Wade Spencer. Are you sure you don't want to wait it out so we can plan accordingly?"

"Everyone we love is here. Why wait?"

"True." Lacey shrugged. "And I do have a wedding planner in the family. Mama, how fast can you whip together a wedding?"

"Are you kidding?" Adelaide shrieked and clapped her hands. "I've had your wedding planned since the day you first drew breath. Say yes, darling, and all you'll have to do is show up."

"No lace," Lacey warned.

"I wouldn't dream of it... Well, I would, but I won't do it. Promise."

Promise lifted her head, her caterpillar eyebrows bouncing up and down at the mention of her name. Lacey giggled. "And speaking of Promise..." Lacey patted her vacant side to invite the dog back up. She sank her fingers into the dog's soft fur at her neck. "Your love is so pure. Your actions are more powerful than any spoken word. Thank you for loving Wade, and showing me how to love him, too." Promise lapped Lacey's face and made her laugh. "I want you by our side when we say I do. It just wouldn't be the same without you."

"So is that a yes?" Wade asked impatiently.

"Wait a second. I don't like to be rushed. Let me think this through."

"You? Since when do think things through? What happened to 'Go unless God tells you no'?"

"About that... I think I might have been a bit too quick with my motto."

"Just a bit?" He smirked, deepening his dimple.

"When the car was filling up, and I had no way of escaping, I realized it wasn't always about going but about letting go."

Wade's smile slipped from his face. He caressed her cheek with the back of his fingers, his eyes glistening with unshed tears. "I'm sorry, Lacey. I won't rush you. If you need time, you take it. As much as you need."

"But I don't. That's just it. My answer is yes, Wade. I will marry you, but I want you to know this is not something I'm rushing into because I haven't heard God say no. I'm walking forward in trust, knowing He is at the lead, and has great plans for us."

Wade sighed and dropped his forehead to hers. "There can't be any regrets in that," he whispered, his voice choked.

"No regrets, only peace."

"Peace." He closed his eyes. "I thought I would be chasing after that forever."

"Well, get used to it. You don't have to search for it anymore."

"Hey," Roni piped up. "Does this mean you're coming home, Wade?"

Wade didn't move from Lacey. "I don't think that's a question for today."

Lacey answered for him. "Yes, he'll be coming home."

Wade lifted his head. "Are you sure about moving north? You're a born-and-bred Southern gal."

"Now who's crazy? You own a racetrack? Hello!" She waved her hand. "We're going to be the greatest racing family ever."

Wade smiled so big his dimple cut into his cheek like a crater. "Racing family? You have no idea what that means to me." He leaned in, his lips a breath from hers. "Start your engine, sweetheart. We've got a legacy ahead of us to claim."

"You know I'm going to spin circles around you, right?"

"I'm counting on it," he said and finally claimed her lips.

Moments went by and Lacey forgot about the people watching. It was easy to do when Wade let all the barriers between them fall away, where it became just the two of them.

It was Michael, Wade's newfound granddaddy, who interrupted. "If you don't mind, I would like to give you your wedding present early, Wade."

Wade stood up from the bed but still held Lacey's hand, his thumb tracing circles on her skin that sent tingles throughout her body. "That's not necessary. Really."

"It is. You've been searching for peace for so long, perhaps I can bring you some. It's what your parents would want me to do. They would be so proud of you. Both of you." He looked to Roni and opened his briefcase. He withdrew a large envelope and handed it to Wade across the bed. "It's the accident report. The real accident report."

"Real?" Both Wade and Roni spoke in unison.

"The one on record was altered. There were certain things I didn't want the public to know. Like I said before, there are people who will hurt my loved ones just to get to me. I could protect you from afar because I knew where you were." Michael sighed and looked to make a quick decision. "But I couldn't protect your brother."

"What are you saying?"

Michael's gaze fell to the envelope. "You'll see in the report that your brother Luke was not found in the car. There were no remains of him at all. Someone removed him from the scene and took him to an unknown place where I couldn't protect him. What I'm saying is, Veronica and Wade, there's a chance your brother is still alive, and out there somewhere."

* * * * *

Dear Reader,

Welcome to a fun new series with the start of *Silent Night Pursuit*. I hope you enjoyed the Spencer siblings and are excited to continue their journey with me down many roads of danger. Look for Roni's story, as well as the baby brother, Luke's, story…if the Spencers can find him.

Both Lacey and Wade had pain to face before they could move forward together. Wade's trauma with his injury of PTSD is felt by so many of our military coming home, experiencing these same wounds. Some have found a service animal to help.

Enter Promise.

Service dogs like her show what unconditional love looks like. In 1 John 3:18, we are instructed not to love with words or tongue but with actions and in truth. Promise's actions were more powerful than any words.

Thanks again for joining me! I love hearing from readers. You can visit my website, www.katyleebooks.com, or email me at katylee@katyleebooks.com. You can also write to me at Katy Lee Books, PO Box 486, Enfield, CT 06082.

Katy Lee